Tess of the d'Urbervilles

黛絲姑娘

商務印書館

This Chinese edition of *Tess of the d'Urbervilles*
has been published with the written permission of
Black Cat Publishing.

The copyright of this Chinese edition is owned by
The Commercial Press (H.K.) Ltd.

Name of Book: Tess of the d'Urbervilles
Author: Thomas Hardy
Retold by: Maud Jackson
Activities: James Tierney
Editor: Alex Smith
Design and art direction: Nadia Maestri
Computer graphics: Sara Blasigh
Picture research: Laura Lagomarsino
Illustrations: Eugène Collilieux
Edition: ©2003 Black Cat Publishing
                an imprint of Cideb Editrice, Genoa, Canterbury

系 列 名：Black Cat 優質英語階梯閱讀 · Level 6
書　　名：黛絲姑娘
責任編輯：傅　伊
封面設計：張　毅
出　　版：商務印書館（香港）有限公司
　　　　　香港筲箕灣耀興道 3 號東滙廣場 8 樓
　　　　　http://www.commercialpress.com.hk
印　　刷：中華商務彩色印刷有限公司
　　　　　香港新界大埔汀麗路 36 號中華商務印刷大廈
版　　次：2004 年 2 月第 1 版第 1 次印刷
　　　　　© 2004 商務印書館（香港）有限公司
　　　　　ISBN 962 07 1697 3
　　　　　Printed in Hong Kong

版權所有　不得翻印

出版説明

　　本館一向倡導優質閱讀，近年來連續推出了以“Q”為標識的 “Quality English Learning 優質英語學習” 系列，其中《讀名著學英語》叢書，更是香港書展入選好書，讀者反響令人鼓舞。推動社會閱讀風氣，推動英語經典閱讀，藉閱讀拓廣世界視野，提高英語水平，已經成為一種潮流。

　　然良好閱讀習慣的養成非一日之功，大多數初、中級程度的讀者，常視直接閱讀厚重的原著為畏途。如何給年輕的讀者提供切實的指引和幫助，如何既提供優質的學習素材，又提供名師的教學方法，是當下社會關注的重要問題。針對這種情況，本館特別延請香港名校名師，根據多年豐富的教學經驗，精選海外適合初、中級英語程度讀者的優質經典讀物，有系統地出版了這套叢書，名為《Black Cat 優質英語階梯閱讀》。

　　《Black Cat 優質英語階梯閱讀》體現了香港名校名師堅持經典學習的教學理念，以及多年行之有效的學習方法。既有經過改寫和縮寫的經典名著，又有富創意的現代作品；既有精心設計的聽、說、讀、寫綜合練習，又有豐富的歷史文化知識；既有彩色插圖、繪圖和照片，又有英美專業演員朗讀作品的 CD。適合口味不同的讀者享受閱讀之樂，欣賞經典之美。

　　《Black Cat 優質英語階梯閱讀》由淺入深，逐階提升，好像參與一個尋寶遊戲，入門並不難，但要真正尋得寶藏，需要投入，更需要堅持。只有置身其中的人，才能體味純正英語的魅力，領略得到真寶的快樂。當英語閱讀成為自己生活的一部分，英語水平的提高自然水到渠成。

商務印書館 (香港) 有限公司

編輯部

使用說明 _____

① **應該怎樣選書？**

按閱讀興趣選書

《Black Cat 優質英語階梯閱讀》精選世界經典作品，也包括富於創意的現代作品；既有膾炙人口的小說、戲劇，又有非小說類的文化知識讀物，品種豐富，內容多樣，適合口味不同的讀者挑選自己感興趣的書，享受閱讀的樂趣。

按英語程度選書

《Black Cat 優質英語階梯閱讀》現設 Level 1 至 Level 6，由淺入深，涵蓋初、中級英語程度。讀物分級採用了國際上通用的劃分標準，主要以詞彙（vocabulary）和結構（structures）劃分。

Level 1 至 Level 3 出現的詞彙較淺顯，相對深的核心詞彙均配上中文解釋，節省讀者查找詞典的時間，以專心理解正文內容。在註釋的幫助下，讀者若能流暢地閱讀正文內容，就不用擔心這一本書程度過深。

Level 1 至 Level 3 出現的動詞時態形式和句子結構比較簡單。動詞時態形式以現在時（present simple）、現在時進行式（present continuous）、過去時（past simple）為主，句子結構大部分是簡單句（simple sentences）。此外，還包括比較級和最高級（comparative and superlative forms）、可數和不可數名詞（countable and uncountable nouns）以及冠詞（articles）等語法知識點。

Level 4 至 Level 6 出現的動詞時態形式，以現在完成時（present perfect）、現在完成時進行式（present perfect continuous）、過去完成時（past perfect continuous）為主，句子結構大部分是複合句（compound sentences）、條件從句（1st and 2nd conditional sentences）等。此外，還包括情態動詞（modal verbs）、被動形式（passive forms）、動名詞（gerunds）、

短語動詞（phrasal verbs）等語法知識點。

　　根據上述的語法範圍，讀者可按自己實際的英語水平，如詞彙量、語法知識、理解能力、閱讀能力等自主選擇，不再受制於學校年級劃分或學歷高低的約束，完全根據個人需要選擇合適的讀物。

② 怎樣提高閱讀效果？

　　閱讀的方法主要有兩種：一是泛讀，二是精讀。兩者各有功能，適當地結合使用，相輔相成，有事半功倍之效。

　　泛讀，指閱讀大量適合自己程度（可稍淺，但不能過深）、不同內容、風格、體裁的讀物，但求明白內容大意，不用花費太多時間鑽研細節，主要作用是多接觸英語，減輕對它的生疏感，鞏固以前所學過的英語，讓腦子在潛意識中吸收詞彙用法、語法結構等。

　　精讀，指小心認真地閱讀內容精彩、組織有條理、遣詞造句又正確的作品，着重點在於理解“準確”及“深入”，欣賞其精彩獨到之處。精讀時，可充分利用書中精心設計的練習，學習掌握有用的英語詞彙和語法知識。精讀後，可再花十分鐘朗讀其中一小段有趣的文字，邊唸邊細心領會文字的結構和意思。

　　《Black Cat 優質英語階梯閱讀》中的作品均值得精讀，如時間有限，不妨嘗試每兩個星期泛讀一本，輔以每星期挑選書中一章精彩的文字精讀。要學好英語，持之以恆地泛讀和精讀英文是最有效的方法。

③ 本系列的練習與測試有何功能？

　　《Black Cat 優質英語階梯閱讀》特別注重練習的設計，為讀者考慮周到，切合實用需求，學習功能強。每章後均配有訓練聽、說、讀、寫四項技能的練習，分量、難度恰到好處。

聽力練習分兩類，一是重聽故事回答問題，二是聆聽主角對話、書信朗讀、或模擬記者訪問後寫出答案，旨在以生活化的練習形式逐步提高聽力。每本書均配有 CD 提供作品朗讀，朗讀者都是專業演員，英國作品由英國演員錄音，美國作品由美國演員錄音，務求增加聆聽的真實感和感染力。多聆聽英式和美式英語兩種發音，可讓讀者熟悉二者的差異，逐漸培養分辨英美發音的能力，提高聆聽理解的準確度。此外，模仿錄音朗讀故事或模仿主人翁在戲劇中的對白，都是訓練口語能力的好方法。

閱讀理解練習形式多樣化，有縱橫字謎、配對、填空、字句重組等等，注重訓練讀者的理解、推敲和聯想等多種閱讀技能。

寫作練習尤具新意，教讀者使用網式圖示（spidergrams）記錄重點，採用問答、書信、電報、記者採訪等多樣化形式，鼓勵讀者動手寫作。

書後更設有升級測試（Exit Test）及答案，供讀者檢查學習效果。充分利用書中的練習和測試，可全面提升聽、說、讀、寫四項技能。

④ 本系列還能提供甚麼幫助？

《Black Cat 優質英語階梯閱讀》提倡豐富多元的現代閱讀，巧用書中提供的資訊，有助於提升英語理解力，擴闊視野。

每本書都設有專章介紹相關的歷史文化知識，經典名著更有作者生平、社會背景等資訊。書內富有表現力的彩色插圖、繪圖和照片，使閱讀充滿趣味，部分加上如何解讀古典名畫的指導，增長見識。有的書還提供一些與主題相關的網址，比如關於不同國家的節慶源流的網址，讓讀者多利用網上資源增進知識。

CONTENTS

First Certificate in English Examination-style exercises

T: GRADE 8 Trinity-style exercises (Grade 8)

Chapters 1, 3, 5, 6, 7 and 10 are recorded.
第1,3,5,6,7,10章錄音

 These symbols indicate the beginning and end of the extracts linked to the listening activities. 聽力練習開始和結束的標記

Thomas Hardy
AND *TESS OF THE D'URBERVILLES*

Thomas Hardy (1893)
by William Strang.

Thomas Hardy (1840-1928) grew up in a Dorset village, surrounded by the countryside that he describes so vividly in *Tess of the d'Urbervilles*. His father was a builder and master mason. [1] Hardy studied architecture, then worked for five years as an architect in London.

A few years before Hardy went to London, in 1859, Darwin's *On the Origin of Species* had been published. Throughout his childhood and early youth, Hardy had been a devout [2] Christian. But, while he was

---

1. **mason** : stone cutter. 2. **devout** : sincerely religious.

9

living in London in the 1860s when intellectual circles were full of debate about the origins of mankind, he began to have serious religious doubts. In 1867 he returned to Dorset, having lost his faith. His first published novel – *Desperate Remedies* – appeared in 1871. From then on he produced a book about every two years for the rest of his life. He published fourteen novels and many volumes of poetry and short stories. His finest novels are *A Pair of Blue Eyes* (1873), *Far from the Madding Crowd* (1874), *The Return of the Native* (1878), *The Mayor of Casterbridge* (1886), *Tess of the d'Urbervilles* (1891), and *Jude the Obscure* (1895). *Tess* is the best known and best loved of all his works.

After *Jude the Obscure*, Hardy stopped writing novels. The poetry that he wrote during the last thirty years of his life is as fine as his fiction, and many modern poets claimed that Hardy was a major influence upon them. He stopped writing novels because of the hostile criticism he had received for the audacious [1] sexual politics [2] of *Tess* and *Jude*. The heroine of *Tess* is a 'fallen woman' [3] and the hero and heroine of *Jude* live together and have children despite the fact that both are married to other people.

The subtitle of *Tess of the d'Urbervilles* is *A Pure Woman*. This outraged [4] many Victorian readers. Tess gave birth to an illegitimate child; therefore, the Victorian readers and reviewers believed, she could not possibly be called a pure woman. One reader burnt the book and sent Hardy the ashes by mail. The subtitle highlights one of the novel's central points: that we should judge people by their

1. **audacious** : fearless.
2. **sexual politics** : ideas and beliefs on sex.
3. **fallen woman** : woman who has had a sexual relationship outside marriage.
4. **outraged** : angered, shocked.

Maxgate Dorchester (*ca.* 1900), the house which Thomas Hardy
designed and lived in until his death in 1928.

intentions rather than by the outward facts of their lives. Hardy
makes it perfectly clear in the novel that Tess does not intend to
submit to [1] Alec d'Urberville's passionate advances. [2] The scene in
The Chase is veiled [3] in mystery. Was Tess raped [4] or seduced? We
are never told clearly, but various details suggest that she was
seduced.

1. **submit to** : accept someone's control.
2. **advances** : (here) attempts to make her sexually interested in him.
3. **veiled** : (here) hidden.
4. **raped** : forced to have sex against her will.

The most subtle [1] and beautiful of these details is a symbolic foreshadowing [2] of the scene in The Chase. It takes place when Tess first meets Alec. He asks her if she likes strawberries, and she replies 'Yes, when they are in season.'

The symbolic parallels, [3] between the strawberry Alec offers her now and the physical love he will offer her later, are clear. But the most interesting aspect of the scene lies in another parallel: that between the strawberry and Tess. Alec asks his question in a greenhouse, [4] a place where ripening [5] is accelerated. It is too early in the season for strawberries, but Alec's greenhouse has rushed the process of ripening. Thus in a subtle and poignant [6] symbolic image, Hardy reminds us that Tess is only seventeen and not yet ready for sexual life.

Tess of the d'Urbervilles is a rich and complex novel, in which Hardy broods on [7] the connections between character and fate. Are social conventions to blame for Tess's tragedy, or was her fate determined by her d'Urberville blood? Sometimes Tess's story seems to be about men's abuse of women and aristocrats' abuse of peasants. At other points it seems a bitter tale written by a man whose faith in a benevolent [8] God had been replaced by belief in a malevolent [9] Fate. Hardy does not give us answers: he asks these vast and disturbing questions and sets them in motion around the simple, appealing, [10] and vulnerable [11] figure of Tess.

1. **subtle** : not easy to describe, fine.
2. **foreshadowing** : warning.
3. **parallels** : similarities.
4. **greenhouse** : a glass building for growing plants.
5. **ripening** : the state of being fully developed.
6. **poignant** : making one sad, full of pity.

1 Answer the following questions.

1. What did Hardy do in London before starting to write?

   ....

2. In the 1860s why did Hardy begin to have religious doubts?

   ....

3. When did Hardy leave London and return to Dorset?

   ....

4. How often did Hardy publish a book? How many novels did he write?

   ....

5. What was the title of Hardy's last novel? How was it similar to *Tess*?

   ....

6. Why did Hardy stop writing novels?

   ....

7. Why were Victorian readers angered by the subtitle *A Pure Woman*?

   ....

8. Alec offered Tess a strawberry in a greenhouse. In what way was this symbolic?

   ....

9. What are some of the questions offered by the novel?

   ....

10. When did Thomas Hardy die?

   ....

7. **broods on** : thinks about unhappily.
8. **benevolent** : kind, friendly.
9. **malevolent** : wishing to do evil.
10. **appealing** : charming.
11. **vulnerable** : that can be hurt or injured.

Before you go on

1 **Think about the following questions.**

The original title of the novel is: *Tess of the d'Urbervilles, A Pure Woman*. What does the subtitle tell us about Hardy's opinion of Tess? How does this compare to public opinion of the time, which you read about in the introduction?

2 **You will hear the first part of Chapter One. For each question, complete the sentence. Then read Chapter One to check your answers.**

Jack Durbeyfield was walking home from Shaston
(**1**).. Marlott.
He met Parson Tringham, who called him (**2**)..............................
....
Jack was (**3**).. to be spoken to like this.
The parson explained that he was (**4**)...
county.
The parson discovered that Jack's ancestors were the
d'Urbervilles, an (**5**)... family.
Jack's ancestor, Sir Pagan d'Urberville was (**6**)............................
.... Normandy with William the Conqueror.
Jack thought this news was (**7**).. .
But he was disappointed to hear that his family was now
(**8**).. .
The d'Urbervilles were all buried at Kingsbere in (**9**)...................
....
Jack decided to go to the (**10**).. to
celebrate.

CHAPTER ONE

Ꝋ NOBLE ꝊAMILY

Ꝋne evening, on his way home from Shaston to the village of Marlott, Jack Durbeyfield met Parson [1] Tringham. 'Good evening, parson,' said Jack.

'Good evening, Sir John.'

Jack looked at the parson in surprise. 'Why do you call me "Sir John"?' he asked. 'You know that I am plain Jack Durbeyfield, the haggler.' [2]

The parson hesitated for a moment, then replied, 'While I was researching the history of this county, I discovered that your ancestors are the d'Urbervilles, an ancient noble family. Your ancestor Sir Pagan d'Urberville was a famous knight who came from Normandy with William the Conqueror.'

'I have never heard it before!'

---

1. **Parson** : an old-fashioned word for a priest.
2. **haggler** : a man who buys and sells goods.

'Yes. Yours is one of the best families in England.'

'How amazing!' cried Jack. 'All these years I thought I was just a common fellow! Tell me, sir, where do we d'Urbervilles live?'

'You don't live anywhere. You are extinct [1]– as a county family.' [2]

'That's bad. But where are we buried?'

'At Kingsbere. Many d'Urbervilles are buried there in marble tombs.'

'And where are our fine houses and our lands?'

'You don't have any, though you once had. Goodnight, Durbeyfield.'

'Well!' thought Jack. 'I'll go to The Pure Drop Pub and have a drink to celebrate this! Then I'll ride home in a carriage!'

END

That evening the women of the village were walking in a procession. It was an old custom. Every year, in the month of May, the women dressed in white and walked together through the village then danced in the field. As they passed by The Pure Drop Pub, one girl called out to another, 'Look, Tess Durbeyfield! There's your father riding home in a carriage!'

Tess turned to look. She was very pretty, with a soft mouth and large innocent eyes. She wore a white muslin [3] dress and a red ribbon in her hair. None of the other girls had a red ribbon.

'Tess!' called her father from the carriage, 'I am descended from [4] a noble family! I have a family vault [5] at Kingsbere!'

---

1. **extinct** : no longer in existence.
2. **county family** : important wealthy family.
3. **muslin** : a fine delicate cotton fabric.
4. **descended from** : having someone as a relative in the distant past.
5. **vault** : a tomb for a noble family.

Tess blushed [1] to see her father make such a fool of himself. 'He's just tired,' she said.

'No!' said the other girl. 'He's drunk!'

'I won't walk with you if you make fun of my father!' cried Tess.

As the carriage drove away, the procession of women entered the field and began to dance.

Three young gentlemen were passing at that moment. They stopped to watch the women dancing. The youngest entered the field.

'What are you doing, Angel?' asked his eldest brother.

'I'm going to dance with them. Why don't we all dance?'

'Don't be foolish. We can't dance with simple country girls. Somebody might see us. Besides, we must get to Stourcastle before dark.'

'Well, you go on. I'll join you in five minutes.'

The two elder brothers – Felix and Cuthbert – walked on.

'Who will dance with me?' Angel asked the women.

'You'll have to choose a partner, sir,' said one of the girls.

Angel looked around and chose the girl nearest to him. He did not choose Tess, even though she was descended from a noble family.

After the dance, Angel noticed Tess. She was standing apart from the others, looking at him sadly. He felt sorry that he had not asked her to dance, but it was too late now. Angel turned and ran down the road after his brothers.

When Tess returned home that evening, she was still thinking

---

1. **blushed** : her face became red with embarrassment.

about the young man who had not asked her to dance. But as soon as she entered the cottage, her father told her what the parson had said. 'I went back to The Pure Drop and told everyone there. One man said there is a lady called Mrs Stoke-d'Urberville living in a fine house near Trantridge. She must be my cousin.'

Mrs Durbeyfield smiled. Her face still had some of the freshness and prettiness of her youth. Tess's good looks came from her mother, not from the noble d'Urbervilles. 'I think you should go and visit her, Tess!' said she. 'I looked in my fortune-telling book and it said you should go!' Tess's mother was a simple country woman who spoke in dialect, sang folk songs, and had many superstitious beliefs. Tess had been educated at the National School and she spoke two languages: dialect at home, and English outside.

Mr and Mrs Durbeyfield had brought nine children into the world. Tess, the eldest, was seventeen. The two after Tess had died in infancy. [1] Then came Liza-Lu, Abraham, two more sisters, a three-year-old boy, and the baby.

Mr Durbeyfield's face was red from drinking. 'I'm tired, Joan,' he said to his wife.

'Father,' said Tess, 'you have to drive the goods [2] to town so we can sell them at the market tomorrow! How will you wake up in time?'

'I'll wake up, don't you worry!' said Jack.

But at two in the morning Joan came to Tess's room. 'I've been trying to wake him, but I can't,' she said. 'If he doesn't leave now, he'll be late for the market!'

'Abraham and I will go,' Tess replied.

---

1. **infancy** : early childhood.

2. **the goods** : (here) things to sell.

Tess loaded the goods onto the cart, [1] which was drawn [2] by Prince, their only horse. Then she and Abraham climbed on and waved goodbye to their mother.

The night sky was full of stars as Tess and Abraham rode along.

'What do you think the stars are?' asked Abraham.

'They are worlds like this one.'

'Really? Are they exactly like our world?'

'No. I think they are like the apples on the tree. Some of them are splendid and healthy but others are rotten.' [3]

'And which are we on – a splendid one or a rotten one?'

'A rotten one.'

They stopped talking, and Tess began to feel sleepy. She tried to stay awake, but in the end she fell asleep. She was woken up by the terrifying sound of an animal in pain. The cart had stopped.

Tess jumped down and saw to her horror that they had crashed into the morning mail-cart in the dark. The pointed wooden shaft [4] of the mail-cart had penetrated [5] Prince's chest like a sword. Tess put her hand on the wound. Prince's blood splashed [6] over her face and dress. The poor horse fell down dead.

'I must go on with the mail,' said the mail-man. 'I'll send someone to help you.'

As Tess and Abraham waited on the road, the sun rose. Then Tess saw the huge pool of blood. 'It's all my fault!' she cried.

---

1. **cart** : a two-wheeled, horse-drawn vehicle.
2. **drawn** : (here) pulled.
3. **rotten** : decayed.
4. **shaft** : the piece of wood that joins the cart to the horse.
5. **penetrated** : pierced.
6. **splashed** : hit, covered.

'How will mother and father get their goods to market without a horse?'

'Is it because we live on a rotten star?' asked Abraham, with tears running down his cheeks. Tess did not reply. Her cheeks were pale and dry, as though she thought herself a murderess.

After Prince's death, life was very difficult for the Durbeyfields. Tess felt responsible for her family's distress [1] and wondered what she could do to help them. One day her mother said, 'Tess, you must go to our cousin Mrs Stoke-d'Urberville and ask for her help. She is very rich.'

Tess took a cart to Trantridge Cross and walked the rest of the way. She passed through The Chase, an ancient forest that had been there for thousands of years. Finally she came to Mrs d'Urberville's house, a fine new mansion known as The Slopes.

Tess was startled [2] and intimidated [3] by the grandeur [4] of The Slopes. The great red-brick house, the green lawn with an ornamental tent on it, the stables: [5] everything about the house and gardens looked like money. 'I thought we were an old family!' thought Tess, 'but this is all new!'

In fact the Stoke-d'Urbervilles were not really d'Urbervilles at all. Mr Simon Stoke had made a fortune as a merchant in the North of England. When he retired, he moved to the South and decided to change his name to something more aristocratic. He looked through a history of the county and found the name

1. **distress** : (here) difficulties, problems.
2. **startled** : (here) surprised.
3. **intimidated** : frightened.
4. **grandeur** : the quality of being large and impressive.
5. **stables** : buildings in which horses are housed.

d'Urberville. So he changed his name to Stoke-d'Urberville. Tess and her family knew nothing about this work of the imagination.

As Tess stood looking at the house, a young man walked out of the ornamental tent, smoking a cigar. He had dark skin, a full mouth, and a black moustache. 'Well, my beauty, what can I do for you?' he asked, looking at Tess boldly. 'I am Mr Alexander d'Urberville. Have you come to see me or my mother?'

Tess was even more surprised by Mr d'Urberville than she was by the house. She had expected her cousins to have fine aristocratic faces, but this man looked almost barbaric. [1] 'I've come to see your mother, sir,' she said.

'You can't see my mother: she is an invalid. [2] Can I help you? What did you wish to discuss with her?'

Tess felt suddenly embarrassed. 'It's so foolish,' she said, smiling shyly. 'I'm afraid to tell you.'

'I like foolish things.'

'I came to tell you that we're of the same family as you.'

'Poor relations?'

'Yes.'

'Stokes?'

'No, d'Urbervilles.'

'Oh, yes. I mean d'Urbervilles.'

'Our name is now Durbeyfield, but we have proof that we are d'Urbervilles. We have an old seal, [3] marked with a lion rampant. And we have an old silver spoon with a castle on it, but it is so worn that mother uses it to stir the soup.'

---

1. **barbaric** : very cruel and violent.
2. **invalid** : a person who has been very ill for a long time and needs to be looked after by others.
3. **seal** : a decorative adhesive stamp.

'A castle argent is certainly my crest,' said he. 'And my arms a lion rampant. [1] And so, you have come on a friendly visit to us, as relations?'

'Yes,' said Tess, looking up again. 'I will go home by the same cart that brought me.'

'The cart won't come for a long time yet. Why not walk with me around the grounds, my pretty cousin?'

Tess wished she could leave immediately, but the young man insisted, so she walked around the grounds with him. He showed her gardens, fruit trees, and greenhouses. In one of the greenhouses, he asked Tess if she liked strawberries.

'Yes,' she replied, 'when they are in season.'

'They are in season here already,' said Alec. He picked a ripe [2] red strawberry and held it to her lips.

'No – no!' she said quickly, putting her fingers between his hand and her lips. 'Please let me take it in my own hand.'

'Nonsense!' [3] he insisted. A little distressed, she parted [4] her lips and took it in.

Alec asked her many questions about herself and her family. She told him about the death of Prince. 'It was all my fault!' she said. 'And now we are even poorer than we were before.'

'Maybe I can do something to help,' said Alec. 'My mother could find work for you here. But if you come to live here, Tess, you mustn't talk nonsense about being a d'Urberville. Your name is Durbeyfield – a completely different name.'

'I wish for no better name, sir,' said Tess with dignity.

1. **castle argent/lion rampant** : the castle argent and lion rampant are the heraldic symbols of the d'Urberville family.
2. **ripe** : ready to be picked and eaten.
3. **Nonsense** : Rubbish.
4. **parted** : (here) opened.

Go back to the text

1 Answer the following questions.

1. Why was Jack celebrating in The Pure Drop pub?
2. Why did Tess blush when she saw her father riding home in a carriage?
3. Where was Tess going when she saw her father in the carriage?
4. When Tess returned home what was she thinking about?
5. Why did Tess and Abraham go to the market and not their father Jack?
6. What was Tess doing when her horse crashed into the mail cart?
7. Were the Stoke-d'Urbervilles really descendants of the original d'Urberville family?
8. What made Mr Simon Stoke decide to change his family name?
9. How did Tess prove to Alexander that the Durbeyfields were really d'Urbervilles?
10. What did Alexander suggest to help improve Tess's financial situation?

2 Complete the table using words from the text. The first one has been completed as an example. Check the spelling of the words in a dictionary.

Noun	Adjective
descendant	descending
nobility	
	superstitious
elegance	
	surprising
extinction	
	aristocratic
fool	
embarrassment	
	difficult

3 Use words from Activity 2 to complete the summary below. For each question, decide if the missing word is a noun or an adjective.

Told by Parson Tringham that he was the (1)................... of a (2)................... family, the d'Urbervilles, Jack Durbeyfield celebrated his good fortune in the local pub. He thought he was part of the (3)................... so he decided to travel home from the pub in an (4)................... carriage. Seeing the carriage pass by, Tess was (5)................... to see her father behaving in such a (6)................... way.

However the d'Urbervilles were not an (7)................... family. In the pub Jack had discovered that living nearby was a family called the Stoke-d'Urbervilles. Mrs Durbeyfield, Tess's mother, was a simple woman, who believed in (8)................... . She encouraged her daughter to visit the Stoke-d'Urbervilles.

Tess was uncertain but did as her parents asked. She believed that the Stoke-d'Urbervilles were an old family. When she arrived at the family home it was a (9)................... for her to see how new everything was. In front of the house she was met by a young man called Alexander. Tess explained how the two families were related. She also told him about the horse and the (10)................... her family faced. Alexander suggested that he could help matters by finding her a job.

Grammar

The Passive

1 Form the passive using: the verb **be** plus the **past participle**.

2 In an active sentence, the subject is the person/thing that does the action. Use an **active** verb to say what the subject **does**.
   *Angel **asked** the girl to dance.*

3 In a passive sentence, the subject of the verb is the person/thing affected by the action. Use a **passive** verb to say what **happens** to the subject.
   *The girl **was asked** to dance.*

4 When we use the passive we can use the agent to show who is the person/thing responsible for the action. If we want to say who does or what causes the action, we use **by**.
*The girl **was asked** to dance **by** Angel.*

4 Read the summary in Activity 3 again and identify three examples of passive forms.

1. ....

2. ....

3. ....

FCE **5** For each question, complete the second sentence using the passive form. Use between 2-5 words. Use the agent only if you think it is important.

1. Jack stared at the parson in a strange way.
   The parson .... by Jack in a strange way.

2. Jack went home from the pub in an elegant carriage.
   Jack was .... pub in an elegant carriage.

3. Somebody said Jack was drunk.
   Jack .... drunk.

4. The girls of the village made fun of Jack.
   Jack was made .... of the village.

5. Jack's behaviour embarrassed Tess.
   Tess .... behaviour.

6. After the dance Angel noticed Tess standing alone.
   Standing apart from the others, Tess .... alone.

7. At the dance Angel chose the girl nearest to him.
   The girl nearest to him .... dance.

8. Tess's mother sings a lot of traditional songs.
   A lot of traditional songs .... mother.

9. The pointed wooden shaft of the mail-cart penetrated Prince's chest.
   Prince's chest .... a pointed wooden shaft.

10. Simon Stoke changed his name to make it sound more aristocratic.
    His name .... more aristocratic.

6 Think about the points below. Use extracts from the text to support your views.

- Describe Tess's relationship with her mother.
- What does Tess think of her father?

7 Write a narrative which describes the accident with the mail-cart from the point of view of the mail-man. Include the following information:

- Where the mail cart had come from
- How the accident happened
- His description of Tess
- Where he went for help

Write your narrative in 120-180 words. Begin like this:

It was very early morning and it was still dark as I drove the mail cart. I watched the road ahead of me carefully. Suddenly...

Before you go on

1 In Chapter Two the handsome Alec d'Urberville meets Tess's family for the first time. He arrived on his horse and he wore 'a diamond ring that glittered every time he put his hand up to his moustache'. Think about these questions:

- Why do you think he put his hand up to his moustache so often?
- What was he trying to demonstrate?
- What do you think Alec d'Urberville will be like?
- What kind of effect do you think he will have on Tess?

CHAPTER TWO

MAIDEN

hen Tess got home the next day, her mother said, 'A letter has come, Tess! Mrs d'Urberville wants you to work on her chicken farm. She says you will have a comfortable room and good wages!' [1]

Tess read the letter, then said, 'I want to stay here with you and father.'

'Why?'

'I don't want to tell you why. I don't really know why.'

For the next few weeks, Tess searched for work close to home, but she found none. One day, when she came home, her mother said, 'Mr d'Urberville came by on his horse and asked if you had decided to work at his mother's chicken farm. Oh, what a handsome man he is!'

1. **wages** : salary.

'I don't think so,' said Tess coldly.

'And he was wearing a diamond ring!' said Abraham. 'I saw it. The diamond glittered [1] every time he put his hand up to his moustache. Why did our rich relation put his hand up to his moustache so often?'

'Perhaps to show his diamond ring,' said Jack.

'Are you going to accept the offer, Tess?' asked her mother.

'Perhaps,' said Tess.

'Well, he likes her,' said Joan to her husband, 'and she should go.'

'I don't like my children going away from home,' said Jack.

'Let her go,' said his poor stupid wife. 'He likes her, and he called her "cousin"! Maybe he'll marry her, and then we will have a new horse and plenty of money!'

'I will go,' said Tess. 'But don't talk about me marrying him. I am going to earn some money so that we can buy a horse.'

Tess wrote to Mrs d'Urberville, accepting her offer. Mrs d'Urberville replied, saying she was glad. Mrs d'Urberville's handwriting seemed rather masculine. [2]

Two days later, the entire family accompanied Tess to meet the cart. As they climbed the hill, the cart appeared on the summit. [3] Tess kissed everyone goodbye and ran up the hill. But then a gig [4] came out from behind the trees.

Tess's face was full of surprise and apprehension [5] as d'Urberville asked her to mount [6] his gig and drive with him to The Slopes. She wanted to ride in the cart. But, when she looked down the hill at her family, she thought about Prince and how she

---

1. **glittered** : shone brightly reflecting the light.
2. **masculine** : with the qualities that people think are typical of men.
3. **summit** : the top of a mountain.
4. **gig** : an elegant two-wheeled, horse-drawn carriage.
5. **apprehension** : worry or fear about something in the future.
6. **mount** : get on.

was responsible for his death. Then she climbed onto the gig with Alec d'Urberville.

As they drove along, Alec paid many compliments to Tess. Joan had insisted that Tess dress in her best clothes. Sitting on the gig in her white muslin dress with a pink ribbon in her hair, Tess wished she had worn her ordinary working clothes. She had a full figure that made her look more of a woman and less of a child than she really was, and the white muslin dress emphasised this. Tess looked out at the green valley of her birth and the grey unfamiliar countryside beyond.

'Will you go slow, sir, when we go downhill?' asked Tess.

'No, Tess,' said d'Urberville, holding his cigar between his strong white teeth and smiling at her. 'I enjoy going down the hills at full gallop!'[1]

As they descended the hill, the gig went faster and faster. The wind blew through Tess's white muslin and chilled her skin.[2] She did not want him to see that she was frightened, but she was afraid of falling off the gig, so she held his arm.

'Don't hold my arm,' said he. 'Hold on around my waist.'

She held his waist, and so they reached the bottom.

'Safe, thank God, in spite of your fooling!'[3] cried Tess.

'Don't be angry, Tess, and don't let go of me now that you are out of danger.'

Tess blushed. She had held onto his waist without thinking.

'Here's another hill! Hang on!'

As the gig sped down the hill, Alec turned to Tess and said,

---

1. **at full gallop** : with the horse running as fast as it can.
2. **chilled her skin** : made her skin cold.
3. **fooling** : behaving in a silly way.

'Now put your arms around my waist as you did before!'

'Never!' cried Tess independently.

'If you let me kiss you, I'll slow down.'

Tess moved as far away from him as she could. 'Will nothing else make you slow down?' she cried.

'Nothing, dear Tess.'

'Oh! All right!'

He slowed the gig down and leaned over to kiss her, but Tess turned her face away.

'You little witch!' cried Alec. 'I'll drive so fast that we will both be killed, if you don't keep your promise.'

'All right!' said Tess, 'but you should be kind to me, since you are my cousin.'

'Nonsense! Come here!'

'I don't want anyone to kiss me, sir!' cried Tess. A big tear rolled down her cheek, and her lips trembled. 'I wish I had stayed at home!'

When d'Urberville kissed her, she blushed with shame. At that moment, Tess's hat blew off in the wind. 'Oh, sir! Let me get my hat!' she said. He stopped the gig. Tess jumped down, ran back along the road, and picked up her hat.

'Come on! Get back on the gig,' said d'Urberville.

'No, sir,' Tess replied. 'I shall walk.'

'You let your hat blow off deliberately!'

Tess did not deny it. D'Urberville began to swear [1] at her. He drove the gig towards her, forcing her to climb into the hedge. [2]

1. **swear** : use words which are rude or offensive.
2. **hedge** : a row of bushes separating the field from the road.

TESS of the
d'URBERVILLES

'You should be ashamed of yourself for using such wicked [1] words!' cried Tess. 'I don't like you at all! I hate you! I'll go back to my mother!'

Alec's anger disappeared at the sight of Tess's. He laughed heartily. [2] 'Well, I like you even more now! Come here, and let there be peace. I won't do it any more against your will, I promise!'

'I won't get back on the gig, sir!' said Tess. She walked along, with the gig moving slowly beside her. In this way they came to The Slopes.

Tess's life at The Slopes was quite pleasant. Her duties were not difficult, and the other workers were friendly. On the first day, Tess was surprised to learn that Mrs d'Urberville was blind. Even so, the old lady was very interested in her chickens and treated them more like pets than farm animals. Every morning Tess brought the chickens to Mrs d'Urberville. The old lady took the chickens in her arms one by one. She recognised each one and called it by its name. Although she was kind and polite to Tess, clearly she had no idea that they were cousins.

Tess often met Alec in the house or the garden. Sometimes it seemed that he was following her, watching her secretly from behind walls and curtains. She was reserved [3] towards him, but he treated her as if they were old friends. He often called her 'cousin', though sometimes his tone was ironic.

On Saturday nights, the villagers went to a nearby market town called Chaseborough to dance, drink beer, and enjoy themselves. At first, Tess refused to go with them, but the others asked her again, and finally she agreed. She enjoyed herself the first time,

1. **wicked** : very bad or evil.
2. **heartily** : cheerfully.
3. **reserved** : slow to show feelings.

so she began to go regularly.

One Saturday in September, Tess worked late at the chicken farm, then walked to Chaseborough alone, because her friends had all gone earlier in the evening. By the time she got there, the sun had already set. At first she could not find her friends, then someone told her that they had gone dancing in the barn [1] of a local farmer. As Tess walked along the road to the barn, she saw Alec standing on the corner.

'Why are you out so late, my beauty?' he said.

She told him she was looking for her friends, so that she could walk home with them.

'I'll see you again,' he called to her as she walked on.

The barn was full of yellow light. Tess's friends were dancing with their arms around each other, like satyrs [2] and nymphs. [3] A young man asked her to dance, but she refused. The dancing seemed so mad and passionate, it made Tess uncomfortable.

'Are any of you walking home soon?' she asked anxiously. She was afraid to walk home alone.

'Oh yes,' replied a man. 'This will be the last dance.'

But when that dance was over, the dancers asked the musicians to play once more. Tess waited and waited.

Suddenly, one of the couples in the dance fell down, and other couples fell on top of them. Tess heard a loud laugh behind her. She looked around and saw the red end of a burning cigar in the shadows. Alec was standing there alone.

'Hello, my beauty. What are you doing here?'

Tess explained that she was waiting for her friends to walk home.

1. **barn** : a large wooden farm-building for storing grain.
2. **satyrs** : gods of the woods, half man and half goat.
3. **nymphs** : minor goddesses living in trees, rivers, hills.

'I'm on horseback this evening, but I could rent a gig from the hotel and drive you home,' he said.

'No, thank you,' she said.

When the dance was finally over, Tess and the others walked back towards Trantridge in the moonlight. Many of the men and some of the women were drunk. Two of the women walked unsteadily: [1] a dark beauty named Car Darch, who was known as the Queen of Spades, and her sister, who was known as the Queen of Diamonds. [2] Until recently, the Queen of Spades had been Alec d'Urberville's favourite.

Car Darch fell in the mud on the road. The others laughed at her, and Tess joined in the laughter. Suddenly Car Darch stood up and said to Tess, 'How dare you laugh at me!'

'Everyone was laughing,' Tess replied.

'You think you are better than the rest of us, just because he likes you best now!'

The Queen of Spades closed her hands and held them up towards Tess, ready to fight.

'I shall not fight you,' said Tess, 'I did not know that you were whores! [3] I wish I had not waited to walk home with you!'

This general comment made the others angry too. The Queen of Diamonds, who had also been one of Alec's favourites in the past, united with her sister against the common enemy. Several other women also insulted Tess. Their husbands and lovers tried to make

---

1. **unsteadily** : with difficulty, likely to fall.
2. **Queen of Spades... Diamonds** : the Queen of Spades and the Queen of Diamonds are two playing cards. Car Darch is called the Queen of Spades because she is a beautiful woman with dark hair. Her sister is called the Queen of Diamonds because she is a beautiful woman with red hair.
3. **whores** : prostitutes.

peace by defending her, but this only made the situation worse.

Tess was no longer afraid to walk home alone, she just wanted to get away from these people. Suddenly Alec appeared on horseback out of the shadows. He rode up to Tess, who was standing a little apart from the others.

'What the devil are you people doing?' he cried. 'Jump up on my horse,' he whispered to Tess, 'and we'll be far away from them in a moment.'

She wanted to refuse his help, as she had refused it before. But now she was afraid of these angry drunken companions. She wanted to mount the horse and ride away, triumphing over [1] her enemies. She gave in to [2] the impulse and got on the horse.

As Alec and Tess rode away, Car Darch and her sister began to laugh.

'What are you laughing at?' asked a young man.

Car's mother, who was also laughing, said, 'Out of the frying-pan into the fire!' [3]

Alec and Tess rode along in silence. Tess was glad of her triumph, but she was nervous about her present situation. She held on [4] to Alec's waist as he rode, because she was afraid of falling off. She asked him to ride slowly, and he did so.

'Are you glad to have escaped from them, dear Tess?' asked Alec.

'Yes. I should be grateful to you.'

'And are you?'

She did not reply.

---

1. **triumphing over** : defeating.
2. **gave in to** : allowed oneself to be defeated by something.
3. **Out of ... fire** : a proverb meaning from a bad situation to a worse one.
4. **held on** : kept her hands on.

'Tess, why do you not like me to kiss you?'

'Because I don't love you.'

'Are you sure?'

'I am angry with you sometimes!'

'Ah, I thought so,' said Alec sadly, but he was not really saddened by what she had said. He knew that any other feeling she had for him was better than indifference. [1]

They fell silent, and the horse walked on. There was a faint luminous [2] fog around them. They had passed the road to Trantridge a long time ago, but Tess had not noticed. She was tired. This morning, as usual, she had risen at five and worked all day. It was now nearly one o'clock. Fatigue [3] overcame [4] her, and her head sank gently against his back.

D'Urberville stopped the horse, turned around, and put his arm around her waist, but the movement woke Tess, and she pushed him away.

'Good God! You nearly pushed me off the horse!' cried Alec.

'I'm sorry, sir,' said Tess humbly.

'For nearly three months you have treated me this way, Tess, and I won't tolerate it! You know that I love you and think you are the prettiest girl in the world, and yet you treat me badly. Will you not let me act as your lover?'

'I don't know – I wish – how can I say yes or no when...'

Then Tess noticed that the road was unfamiliar. 'Where are we?' she asked.

'We are in The Chase – the oldest forest in England. It's a

1. **indifference** : absence of feeling.
2. **luminous** : shining in the dark.
3. **fatigue** : great tiredness.
4. **overcame** : defeated.

lovely night, and I thought we could ride for a little longer.'

'How could you be so treacherous! [1] Let me down. I want to walk home.'

'You cannot walk home, darling. We are miles from Trantridge.'

'Never mind. Let me down, sir!'

'All right,' said Alec. 'But I don't know where we are. Promise to wait by the horse while I walk through the woods in search of a road or a house. When I know where we are, I will give you directions and let you walk home alone, or you may ride, if you wish.'

Tess agreed to this plan.

Alec tied [2] the horse to a tree and made a pile of [3] dried leaves on the ground nearby. 'Sit there,' he said. 'I'll be back soon. By the way, Tess, somebody gave your father a new horse today.'

'How very kind of you!' she cried, but she felt embarrassed having to thank him at that moment. 'I almost wish that you had not.'

'Why, dear?'

'It makes things difficult for me.'

'Tessy – don't you love me a little now?'

'I'm grateful,' she reluctantly admitted. 'But I don't love you.'

The knowledge that his passion for her had caused him to be so kind to her family made Tess feel sad, and she began to cry.

'Don't cry, dear! Sit down here and wait for me. Are you cold?'

Tess was wearing only her thin muslin dress. Alec took off his coat and put it over her shoulders, then he walked off into the fog.

---

1. **treacherous** : disloyal and deceiving.
2. **tied** : attached with a piece of rope.
3. **pile of** : large amount, all lying one on top of the other.

He went up the hill so that he could see the surrounding countryside and discover where they were. From the hilltop he saw a familiar road, so he turned back. The moon had now set, [1] and The Chase was dark. At first he could not find the spot [2] where he had left the horse. But, after walking around in the darkness for some time, he heard the sound of the horse moving.

'Tess?'

There was no answer. It was so dark that he could see nothing but the pale cloud of her dress on the ground at his feet. He stooped [3] and heard her gentle regular breathing. He knelt beside her and bent lower till her breath warmed his face and his cheek rested on hers. She was asleep, and there were tears on her eyelashes.

The ancient trees of The Chase rose high above them in darkness and silence. But where was Tess's guardian angel? This coarse [4] young man was about to claim [5] a fine, sensitive, pure girl for his own. Why does this happen so often? Perhaps in this case Nemesis [6] was involved. No doubt some of Tess's noble ancestors had treated the peasant girls of their time in the same way.

Tess's own people, who believe in Fate, [7] often say, 'It was to be.' [8] That was the pity of it.

---

1. **set** : (here) moved below the horizon.
2. **spot** : (here) place.
3. **stooped** : bent down.
4. **coarse** : rude.
5. **claim** : (here) take.
6. **Nemesis** : god of retributive justice, righteous anger and divine vengeance, also god of night.
7. **Fate** : Destiny.
8. **It was to be** : it was predetermined; it was destined to happen.

Go back to the text

1 **Answer the following questions.**

1. Why did Tess decide to take the job on the chicken farm?
2. Why did Tess wish she had worn her ordinary clothes?
3. What made the Queen of Spades want to fight with Tess?
4. How did Tess react when Alec d'Urberville kissed her?
5. Why did Car's mother use the expression, 'Out of the frying pan into the fire'?
6. What reason did Alec give for passing the road to Trantridge?
7. In what way had Alec been kind to Tess's family?
8. How did Tess react to this news?
9. Why did Alec walk up the hill?
10. What is meant by the question, 'Where was Tess's guardian angel?'

2 **How do we travel? Put a tick in the correct box to show which verb goes with which noun.**

	carriage	horse	car	bicycle	bus	plane
get in	✓	✗	✓	✗	✗	✗
ride						
get on						
drive						
miss						
catch						

3 **Complete the sentences below using the word combinations in Activity 2.**

1. There were so many passengers that it took ages to .... the plane.
2. The traffic was so heavy that we .... the train.

3. At the weekend I like to .... my mountain bike.

4. It was difficult for all six of us to .... the car.

5. I really must go now. I have to .... a train at six.

6. It must be difficult to .... a bus in a crowded city centre.

4 Complete the sentences below using the prepositions in the box. There is one extra preposition that you do not need to use. Some words can be used more than once.

> about   around   by   in
> of   off   on   up

1. Tess wanted to ride .... Alec's carriage.

2. Tess put her hands .... his waist.

3. Tess's hat blew .... in the wind.

4. She ran back along the road and picked .... the hat.

5. Mrs d'Urberville was very interested .... chickens.

6. She called each chicken .... its name.

7. Tess saw Alec standing .... the corner.

8. Tess was afraid .... walking home alone.

9. Afraid of the drunken whores Tess got .... the horse.

10. Tess rode in silence, she was nervous .... her present situation.

Grammar

Past Simple and Past Continuous – Revision

The **Past Simple** is used to describe a finished action in the past.
*Tess **wrote** to Mrs d'Urberville to accept her offer.*

The **Past Continuous** is used to describe an action in progress in the past.
*Sometimes it seemed that he **was following** her.*

Using **as**, the **Past Simple** can be used to describe two simultaneous actions in the past.
*As d'Urberville **kissed** her, Tess **blushed** with shame.*

Using **as** or **while**, the **Past Simple** and **Past Continuous** can be used together when one shorter action happens at the same time as a longer action.
*As Alec **was walking** (longer action) around in the darkness, he **heard** (shorter action) the sound of the horse.*

5 Use the Past Simple of the verbs in brackets to join together two simultaneous actions from the text.

1. As they (*drive*) along
2. As they (*descend*) the hill
3. As Tess (*walk*) along the road
4. As they (*ride*) together on the horse
5. As Alec (*climb*) the hill
6. As Alec and Tess (*ride*) away

A Tess (*hold*) his waist.
B Car Darch and her sister (*begin*) to laugh.
C Tess (*wait*) for him.
D Alec (*pay*) Tess many compliments.
E the gig (*go*) faster and faster.
F she (*see*) Alec on the corner.

6 Past Simple or Past Continuous? Complete the sentences below using *as* or *while* and one long action (Past Continuous) and one short action (Past Simple).

1. he/the beach/on/work/lie/she
....
2. to rain/start/for/wait/I/the bus
....
3. they/down/see/walk/the street/an accident
....
4. listen/we/home/the radio/drive/last night
....

5. the house/the alarm/enter/go off/I

   ....

6. the check in/our/be/at/take off/we/plane

   ....

7 At the end of Chapter One, you were asked to discuss Alec d'Urberville. Has your opinion of Alec changed? What do you think Alec represents in Hardy's novel? How would you describe Tess's situation?

8 In Chapter Two, there are many images of life in the country in Victorian England. Make a list of these images or underline them. What do you think life was like for the farm workers?

9 Imagine you are Tess. Write a letter to Mrs d'Urberville accepting her offer of a job on the chicken farm. In your letter, you should use paragraphs and say:

Paragraph 1
- Why the job is important for you and your family
- Explain about the accident with the horse

Paragraph 2
- How surprised you are to find that you have relatives
- Ask about the family

Paragraph 3
- Your intention to work hard
- Ask about the house and the kind of work which is done there

Write your letter in 120-180 words.

Before you go on

1 At the beginning of Chapter Three, Tess is looking at the valley where she was born and thinks, 'Since she had last seen it, she had learned that the serpent hisses where the sweet birds sing, and her views of life had been totally changed by the lesson.' What do you think Hardy means?

2 In Chapter Three Tess tells her mother what happened between her and Alec. Was this a good or bad idea? How do you think her mother will react? What do you think will happen to Tess in Chapter Three?

FCE 3 Listen to the first part of Chapter Three. For each question, decide if the statement is true (T) or false (F).

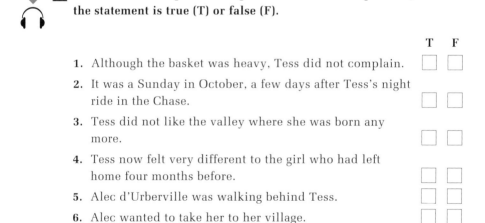

	T	F
1. Although the basket was heavy, Tess did not complain.	☐	☐
2. It was a Sunday in October, a few days after Tess's night ride in the Chase.	☐	☐
3. Tess did not like the valley where she was born any more.	☐	☐
4. Tess now felt very different to the girl who had left home four months before.	☐	☐
5. Alec d'Urberville was walking behind Tess.	☐	☐
6. Alec wanted to take her to her village.	☐	☐

CHAPTER THREE

MAIDEN NO MORE

he basket was heavy, but she carried it without complaining: her heaviest burdens [1] were not material things. It was a Sunday morning in late October, a few weeks after Tess's night ride in The Chase. She climbed the hill and looked down into the valley of her birth. Today it seemed even more beautiful than usual. Since she had last seen it, she had learned that the serpent hisses where the sweet birds sing, and her views of life had been totally changed by the lesson. She was now a different girl from the one who had left her home four months earlier.

Alec drove up behind her in a gig. 'Why did you run away?' he asked. 'I had to drive very fast to catch up with you. If you won't come back to Trantridge with me, at least let me take you to your

---

1. **burdens** : loads, things she had to carry.

village in the gig.'

'I won't come back.'

'Let me take you home then.'

She put her basket and bundle [1] in the gig and climbed up beside him. She had no fear of him now, and the reason for that was also the cause of her sorrow.

Alec had quite forgotten his struggle to kiss her in June, when they had driven together along the same road in the opposite direction. She had not forgotten, and now she sat with her head down, replying to his remarks in monosyllables. [2]

When the village of Marlott came in sight, Tess began to cry.

'Why are you crying?' he coldly asked.

'I was born there.'

'Well – we were all born somewhere.'

'I wish I had never been born!'

'If you didn't want to come to Trantridge, why did you come? I know you didn't come because you loved me!'

'No, I did not go there because I loved you – I never sincerely loved you. That is why I hate myself for my weakness! I didn't understand your meaning [3] until it was too late.'

'That's what every woman says.'

'How dare you use such words!' she cried, turning to him with a flash of anger. 'Don't you know that what every woman says some women may feel?'

'All right. I admit that I did wrong. But I'm willing to pay for

1. **bundle** : a lot of things tied together.
2. **monosyllables** : words with only one syllable.
3. **meaning** : (here) intention.

it. You don't need to work ever again. You can buy yourself beautiful clothes.'

'I don't want your money!'

'Well, if you need anything in the future, write to me, and I'll send it to you.'

He stopped the gig and helped her down. They were at the edge [1] of the village now, and she wanted to walk the rest of the way alone. 'Let me kiss you goodbye, Tess,' he said.

'If you wish.' She stood there passively while he kissed first one cheek and then the other.

'You never let me kiss your mouth, though, and you never kiss me back. I'm afraid you'll never love me.'

'No. I'll never love you. Perhaps I should lie about that now. But I have a little honour left, and so I won't tell that lie.'

'Then goodbye, dear cousin,' he said. He leapt [2] onto the gig and was gone.

As Tess walked along the country lane to Marlott, she passed a man who was writing texts from the Bible in bold red paint on a wall. He had already completed one that read, *Thy damnation slumbereth not.* [3] Now he was writing another: *Thou shalt not commit... .* Against the soft blues and greys of the landscape, the scarlet letters seemed grotesque, [4] and their message seemed frightening and horrible.

Then she saw the smoke rising from the chimney of her old

1. **edge** : (here) beginning.
2. **leapt** : moved quickly.
3. ***Thy ... not*** : your damnation is not sleeping; your sins will be punished.
4. **grotesque** : strange.

home, and her heart ached. [1]

'My dear!' cried her mother, when Tess appeared at the kitchen door. 'Have you come home to be married to your cousin?'

'No,' said Tess quietly. 'He is not my cousin, and he will not marry me.'

'For a holiday, then?'

'Yes.'

Her mother looked at her closely. 'What has happened?' she asked. Tess rested her head against her mother's shoulder and told her everything.

'And yet you didn't get him to marry you!'

'Any woman except me,' said Tess.

'Why didn't you think of your family, instead of thinking only of yourself? Your father is not well, and you see how hard I work. He gave us the horse and many other presents. If he is not your cousin, he must have done it because he loves you. And yet you didn't get him to marry you! You should have been more careful, if you did not want to be his wife.'

'O mother!' cried poor Tess. 'How could I have known? Why didn't you tell me that men were dangerous? Why didn't you warn me?'

Joan said, 'I did not want you to be afraid and lose your chance. Ah, well! We must make the best of it. [2] It is nature, after all. It pleases God!'

Rumours [3] of her wealthy cousin's love for her made other girls

---

1. **ached** : felt a dull constant pain.
2. **make the best of it** : endure it, and try to see the positive side of it.
3. **rumours** : gossip.

TESS of the
d'URBERVILLES

in the village admire and envy [1] Tess. As time went by, however, she began to hate the way they looked at her and talked about her in whispers. [2] She left the house less and less frequently. If she wanted to take a walk, she went at dusk, [3] when most people were at home.

During those walks, Tess often saw the birds and the rabbits in the trees and hedges. She felt different from them. She felt that she was Guilt walking through the places of Innocence; but she was wrong to think that. She had been made to break an accepted social law, but she had broken no law of nature.

---

1. **envy** : feel jealous of.
2. **whispers** : (here) gossip which Tess couldn't hear.
3. **dusk** : the end of the day.

Go back to the text

1 Decide if the following statements are true (T) or false (F).

		T	F
1.	As Tess climbed the hill, the valley seemed unchanged.	☐	☐
2.	After what happened in the Chase, Tess was afraid of Alec.	☐	☐
3.	Riding in the gig, Alec was sensitive towards Tess's sadness.	☐	☐
4.	Alec acknowledged that he was wrong to force himself on Tess.	☐	☐
5.	Tess responded emotionally as Alec kissed her on the cheeks.	☐	☐
6.	Reading the texts from the Bible, Tess felt better.	☐	☐
7.	Tess explained to her mother what had happened.	☐	☐
8.	Joan thought that marrying Alec was a good opportunity.	☐	☐
9.	Tess was pleased to be the envy of the girls in the village.	☐	☐
10.	Walking alone in the woods, Tess regained a sense of innocence.	☐	☐

2 Find words in Chapter Three that have the opposite meanings to the words below.

0. laugh	*cry*	4. single	....
1. lightest	....	5. despise	....
2. spiritual	....	6. rarely	....
3. happiness	....	7. innocence	....

3 Now think of words with similar meanings to the words found in the text.

0. cry	*weep*	4.	....
1.	....	5.	....
2.	....	6.	....
3.	....	7.	....

Grammar

Reported Speech

1 When you change from Direct Speech to Reported Speech, the verb changes tense. It 'jumps' one tense back.

Compare:	Direct	Reported
	*'I **like** football.'*	*Tom said he **liked** football.*
	*'I**'m having** a party.'*	*She said she **was having** a party.*
	*'He **has** never **learnt** to drive.'*	*He said he **had** never **learnt** to drive.*
	*'I **went** to the Hardy Museum.'*	*He said he **had been** to the Hardy Museum.*
	*'They **had** just **arrived**.'*	*She said that they **had** just **arrived**.*
	*'**Can** you drive?'*	*Alison asked if he **could** drive.*
	*'I **might** come.'*	*He said he **might** come.*

Note: The Past Perfect and some modal verbs, e.g. **might**, stay the same.

2 Don't forget to change the word order in questions and use **if**, if the question has a **yes/no** answer.

3 It is not necessary to change the verb if what you report is **still** true.

Compare:	Direct	Reported
	*New York **is** a big city.*	*She said New York **is** a big city.*

4 **For each question, complete the second sentence using either direct or reported speech.**

1. She said that she wouldn't come back.
   '...,' said Tess.

2. Tess explained that she hadn't gone there because she loved him.
   'No, ...,' said Tess.

3. Tess said that she didn't want his money.
'..,' said Tess to Alec.

4. Joan asked why Tess hadn't thought of her family.
'Why ....?' asked Joan.

5. Joan said that Tess should have been more careful.
'..,' said Joan to Tess.

6. 'Why did you run away?'
Alec asked ....

7. 'I wish I had never been born.'
Tess said ....

8. 'I'll never love you.'
Tess said ....

9. 'Have you come home to be married?'
Tess's mother asked if ....

10. 'Why didn't you warn me?'
Tess asked her mother ....

5 Tess decides to leave her job. Imagine you are Tess. Write a letter to Mrs d'Urberville explaining why you have decided to leave. You *don't* want to tell her what has really happened. Use examples of reported speech where possible. You should say:

- Your father is ill. As the eldest child, you are needed at home.
- Your mother needs help taking goods to market.
- There is a new horse and lots of different jobs to do.
- The other children need to be looked after.
- Thank Mrs d'Urberville for her kindness in offering you the job.

Write your letter in 120-180 words. Begin like this:

Dear Mrs d'Urberville,

I am very sorry to tell you that today I received a letter from home. It brings bad news about my father. ...

6 At the end of Chapter Three, Tess is pregnant and alone. Make a list of Tess's descriptions or underline them. What kind of impression do they create? What do you think Tess will do when the baby is born? Consider the following points:

- Where will they live?
- Will Tess work or stay at home?
- Who will look after the baby?

Before you go on

FCE **1** Read the first part of Chapter Four below. For each question, think of the word which best fits each space. Then read Chapter Four to check your answers.

It was a (1).................... morning in August. As the sun rose, the morning mists evaporated. On such a morning it was (2)................... to understand the ancient sun worshippers. There has never (3).................... a saner religion! The sun was a golden-haired god, vigorous and young, looking down (4).................... the earth with loving interest. His light broke through the cottage windows and awoke those still sleeping. The brightest thing the sun illuminated (5).................... morning was the great reaping-machine that stood in the corn (6).................... . Soon a group (7).................... field-workers came down the lane and entered the field. A strange sound came (8).................... of the machine, and it began to (9).................... slowly. The mechanical reaper passed down the hill and out of sight. In a minute it came up on the (10).................... side of the field. As the machine went round, it (11).................... the corn. Each time it completed a circuit, the area of standing corn left in the middle of the field was (12).................... . Rabbits, snakes, rats, and mice ran towards the centre of the field.
The reaping-machine left (13).................... it piles of corn, and the field-workers followed it, tying the corn (14).................... sheaves. The women were more (15).................... to watch than the men. A field-man is a personality in the field; a field-woman is a part of the field. Somehow she loses her own boundaries; she absorbs the essence of the landscape and (16).................... part of it.

CHAPTER FOUR

ȘORROW

t was a warm morning in August. As the sun rose, the morning mists evaporated.[1] On such a morning it was easy to understand the ancient sun worshippers. There has never been a saner[2] religion! The sun was a golden-haired god, vigorous and young, looking down on the earth with loving interest. His light broke through the cottage windows and awoke those still sleeping. The brightest thing the sun illuminated that morning was the great reaping-machine[3] that stood in the corn field. Soon a group of field workers came down the lane and entered the field. A strange sound came out of the machine, and it began to move slowly. The mechanical reaper passed down the hill and out of sight. In a minute it came up on the other side of the field. As the machine went round, it cut the corn. Each time it completed a circuit, the

1. **evaporated** : changed into gas and disappeared.
2. **saner** : more reasonable, sensible.
3. **reaping-machine** : a machine for cutting the corn.

area of standing corn left in the middle of the field was smaller. Rabbits, snakes, rats, and mice ran towards the centre of the field.

The reaping-machine left behind it piles of corn, and the field workers followed it, tying the corn into sheaves. [1] The women were more interesting to watch than the men. A field man is a personality in the field; a field woman is a part of the field. Somehow she loses her own boundaries; she absorbs the essence [2] of the landscape and becomes part of it.

The field women wore hats to protect them from the sun and gloves to prevent their hands from being scratched [3] by the stubble. [4] One was wearing a pale pink jacket, another wore a beige dress, and a third had a bright red skirt. The girl in the pale pink jacket was the most interesting. She had the finest figure of all the women there, and her manner was the most reserved. The other women often looked around them, but Tess never raised her eyes from her work.

She tied the sheaves of corn with clock-like monotony. [5]

At eleven o'clock the field workers paused for lunch. Tess's sisters and brothers brought her lunch and the baby. Tess took the baby from her sister, unfastened [6] the front of her dress, and began suckling [7] the child.

When the baby had finished feeding, Tess held it in her arms and looked off into the distance with a sad indifference that was almost dislike. Then suddenly she started kissing the baby with

1. **sheaves** : (here) piles, or rolls, of corn which have been tied together.
2. **essence** : the basic quality of something.
3. **scratched** : cut or damaged on the surface.
4. **stubble** : (here) the ends of the plants left after the corn has been cut.
5. **monotony** : lack of variety that causes boredom.
6. **unfastened** : loosened.
7. **suckling** : breast-feeding.

passionate intensity.

'She loves that child,' said the woman in the red skirt, 'even though she says she wishes that both she and the baby had died.'

'Oh,' said the woman in the beige dress. 'She'll get used to it! You get used to anything in time!'

'Some people say they heard a woman crying in The Chase one night last year!'

'What a shame!'

When lunchtime was over, Tess gave the baby to her sister, put on her gloves, and went back to work. All afternoon and evening she continued to bind [1] the sheaves of corn. Then, as the moon rose over the fields, she went back to the village with the other workers. The field women sang songs on the way. One of them invented a new verse about a maid who went into the forest and came back in a changed state. As she sang it, the others smiled at Tess. Touched by the women's friendliness, Tess began to feel a little happier.

When she got home that evening, the baby was ill. This was not surprising: he had been small and weak from birth. Tess was frightened because he had not been baptised. [2]

The family went to sleep, but Tess lay anxiously awake. In the middle of the night, the baby got worse. The clock struck one, that hour when imagination is stronger than reason and malignant [3] possibilities become realities. She imagined the Devil sticking his trident [4] into her baby. The image frightened her so much that she cried out loud: 'O, merciful God, have pity on my poor baby! Be

1. **bind** : put or tie together.
2. **baptised** : christened.
3. **malignant** : showing great desire to harm others.
4. **trident** : spear with three points.

angry with me, but pity the poor child!'

Then suddenly she had an idea: She lit a candle then went to the other beds in the room and woke her brothers and sisters. She poured some water into the washbasin. She made her brothers and sisters kneel with their hands together in prayer. The children, still half asleep, were full of awe [1] as they watched their sister take her baby from its bed. Tess then stood erect with the baby on her arm. Liza-Lu, the eldest after Tess, held the Prayer Book open. Thus Tess baptised her own child.

Her figure looked tall and imposing [2] as she stood in her long white nightgown. In the gentle candlelight, her eyes flashed with enthusiasm. Her motherhood [3] – which had been her shame – now seemed transfigured [4] into something of immaculate [5] beauty, touched with a dignity that was almost regal. [6] The children looked up at her in awe.

Tess had decided to name the child Sorrow. Now, as she proceeded with the baptismal service, she pronounced it: 'SORROW, I baptise you in the name of the Father, and of the Son, and of the Holy Spirit.'

She dropped some water on his head.

'Say "Amen", children.'

'Amen,' said the children obediently.

As she read out the baptismal service, Tess's voice became stronger and more passionate, and her face shone with faith.

In the blue of the morning, poor Sorrow died.

1. **awe** : feeling of respect mixed with fear and mystery.
2. **imposing** : impressive.
3. **motherhood** : state of being a mother.
4. **transfigured** : changed her appearance.
5. **immaculate** : perfect.
6. **regal** : like a queen.

Go back to the text

1 Answer the following questions.

1. How many months had passed between the beginning of Chapter Three and the beginning of Chapter Four?
2. What were two effects of the sun at the beginning of the chapter?
3. What kind of protective clothing did the field women wear and why?
4. Who brought lunch for Tess and the baby?
5. One of the field women used the expression, 'What a shame.' What did she mean by this?
6. Why did Tess feel happier on the way home after work?
7. Describe the physical condition of the baby using examples from the text.
8. Why was Tess afraid when the baby became ill?
9. Why did Tess light the candle?
10. During the baptism, why did Tess's voice become stronger and more passionate?

2 Match these verb-noun collocations from the text. One has been completed as an example.

Verb
1. unfasten
2. enter
3. feel
4. sing
5. baptise
6. look
7. light
8. wear
9. tie
10. raise

Noun
A. child
B. candle
C. corn
D. dress
E. field
F. hat
G. eyes
H. happy
I. song
J. tall

3 Choose from the collocations above to complete these sentences from the text. For each question, use the correct tense.

0. The field women sang songs on the way home.

1. A group of workers came down the lane and ....

2. The women followed the reaping machine, ...
into sheaves.

3. The women .... to protect them from the sun.

4. Tess never .... from her work.

5. Tess took the child from her sister, ..., and
began suckling the child.

6. Tess began .... happier.

7. She ...., then went to the other beds in the room
and woke her brothers and sisters.

8. Her figure .... and imposing as she stood in her
long white night-gown.

4 Do you think that the baptism of the baby was a positive or negative experience for Tess? Use words or phrases from the text to support your opinion.

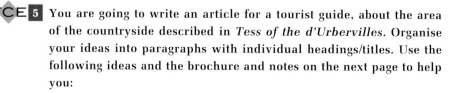 **5** You are going to write an article for a tourist guide, about the area of the countryside described in *Tess of the d'Urbervilles*. Organise your ideas into paragraphs with individual headings/titles. Use the following ideas and the brochure and notes on the next page to help you:

* General description of the place – villages, fields and colours
* Links with Thomas Hardy
* Things to do and see
* Opinion of the place

Come and visit Dorset

Thomas Hardy country!

Come to this beautiful corner of England. You will find unspoilt countryside, beautiful beaches, country market towns and quiet villages.

Take advantage of our *Thomas Hardy Tour* of the valleys and villages in Dorset associated with the great writer.

You can do anything you like in Dorset! Choose from:

• walking on the beautiful hills above the villages
• cycling on the country roads
• fishing in the lakes and rivers, and on the coast
• sunbathing on wonderful sandy beaches
• golfing at eleven golf courses
• horse riding at the riding centres in Abbotsbury or Bridport
• eat in great restaurants and drink in historic pubs

The weather in the South West of England is generally drier and warmer than the rest of the country. But, it can change very quickly, so bring a coat or an umbrella! There are a variety of places to stay from luxurious 5 ***** hotels to campsites

Visit us at www.ThomasHardyCountry.net or visit us next year in Dorset!

Dorchester is in many of Hardy's novels, for example 'Jude the Obscure'. Hardy came to live here in 1885, in a house called Max Gate, which he designed himself, died here in 1928.

The tour goes to the church in West Stafford where Tess and Angel Clare were married, the town of Bere Regis where the d'Urbervilles were buried, the village of Cerne Abbas featured in 'Tess', also Higher Brockhampton, where Hardy was born in 1840.

Lyme Regis very good for sea fishing, nice beach here too

great beach at Weymouth

The website www.b&b.net is very good for bed and breakfast accommodation on farms etc.

Now write the letter to your friend in 120-180 words.

Before you go on

1 In Chapter Five Tess decides to leave Marlott. On her way to a new job in Stourcastle, she passes Kingsbere Church, the burial place of the d'Urbervilles. Is Tess's tragedy an accident or her fate because she is descended from a noble family? Find evidence from the text to support your ideas. How do you think Tess felt towards her ancestors?

T: GRADE 8

2 Topic – The world of work
In Chapter Five Tess goes to find work on a dairy farm. Choose a picture or object which shows a job you would like to do. Use the following questions to help you.

a. What does the picture show/is the object for?

b. What is the job? Why would you like to do it?

c. What would be the duties you do in this job?

d. What would be the advantages and disadvantages of doing this job?

e. Would you prefer to work in the city or the country?

3 You will hear the first part of Chapter Five. For each question, complete the sentences. Then read Chapter Five to check your answers.

Tess stayed with her family through the (**1**)...................................
months. She was not a (**2**)................................... any more.
She was now a (**3**)................................... .
Her (**4**)................................... had not been demoralised by
(**5**)................................... . Spring moved Tess with a
(**6**)................................... . She would never (**7**)...................................
Marlott again. Tess (**8**)................................... that a dairy farm
(**9**)................................... needed a milkmaid. The spirit of youth
was rising in her and with it came (**10**)................................... .

63

CHAPTER FIVE

THE DAIRY

ess stayed with her family all through the winter months. Her experiences had changed her from a simple girl to a complex woman. Her soul was that of a woman who had not been demoralised [1] by her sorrows.

The spring came, with a feeling of germination [2] in the air. It moved Tess with a desire for life. She knew that she could never be comfortable in Marlott again. But if she went somewhere else, where no one knew her history? Tess longed [3] to go. She heard that a dairy farm many miles to the south needed a milkmaid, and she decided to go there. A spirit was rising in her as automatically as the sap [4] in the trees: it was the spirit of youth, and with it came hope.

END

---

1. **demoralised** : disheartened.
2. **germination** : the state of seeds starting growing.
3. **longed** : wanted very much, desired.
4. **sap** : the liquid which carries food in trees.

On a beautiful morning in May, she took a hired cart to the town of Stourcastle. There she took another cart to Talbothay's Dairy. The cart passed by Kingsbere Church, where the d'Urbervilles were buried. Tess no longer admired her ancestors. They were responsible, she felt, for all her troubles. 'I will tell no one in the new place that I am a d'Urberville,' she thought. Yet one of the reasons this particular place attracted her was that it was near the ancestral lands of her family.

She looked with interest as the cart entered the Valley of the Great Dairies, a verdant [1] plain watered by the River Froom. 'This will be my new home!' she thought. The green fields were full of brown and white cattle, grazing [2] peacefully in the evening light. The waters of the River Froom were clear and rapid. Tess felt happy and hopeful. The fresh air and the excitement of a new place made her cheeks pink and her eyes bright.

She reached the dairy at milking-time. The dairy workers in the milk-house [3] watched with interest as Tess approached. The owner of the dairy – Mr Crick – introduced himself to Tess. 'Do you want something to eat before you start milking?' he asked.

'No, thank you,' Tess replied. Mr Crick gave her a stool. She placed it beside a cow, sat down, rested her cheek against the cow's side, and began milking. Soon the only sound in the milk-house was that of warm milk squirting [4] into buckets.

After a little while, the dairy workers began to talk.

'The cows are not giving as much milk as usual,' said one.

---

1. **verdant** : fresh and green.
2. **grazing** : eating grass.
3. **milk-house** : the building in which the cattle are milked.
4. **squirting** : (here) the quick movement of the milk coming from the cow, coming out as a jet of liquid.

'That's because we have someone new in the dairy,' replied another. 'It always happens.'

'We should sing a song to calm their nerves,' said a third.

'You could play your harp to them, sir,' said Mr Crick.

'Why?' asked a voice that seemed to come from the brown cow opposite Tess.

Then a dairy-worker told a story about a man being chased [1] by a bull. The man had his fiddle [2] with him, and he played music to calm the bull. The bull stood still. Then the man played a Christmas song, and the bull got down on his knees.

'What a strange story!' said the voice from behind the brown cow. 'It is like a story from medieval times, when faith was a living thing!'

Tess wondered who the speaker was. Why did the others call him 'sir'? Finally he stood up. 'I think I have finished this one,' he said. 'Though she made my fingers ache.'

Tess could now see him. He wore the usual clothes of a dairyman, but there was something educated, reserved, sad, and different about him. Suddenly she realised that she had seen him before. He was the young gentleman who had not asked her to dance in the field at Marlott that day, so long ago, before all her troubles began.

That night Tess went to bed in a large room over the milk-house, which she shared with three other milkmaids. Retty, who had the bed next to Tess, kept talking about Talbothay's and all the people there: 'That young gentleman – the one who is learning to milk and plays the harp – is Mr Angel Clare. He's a parson's

---

1. **chased** : ran after.
2. **fiddle** : violin.

son. His father is the Reverend Clare at Emminster. His brothers will become parsons like their father, but Mr Angel wants to be a farmer.'

Tess was too tired to ask her neighbour questions. Gradually she fell asleep to the sound of her voice and the smell of the cheeses stored in the cheese-room next door.

Angel was the youngest and brightest [1] of the Reverend Clare's three sons. But he had disappointed his father. The Reverend Clare had wished all three of his sons to become parsons like himself, but Angel had refused.

'Father, I do not want to join the clergy,' he had said one day. 'I love the Church as one loves a parent, but I have doubts about several of her doctrines.'

'If you refuse to join the clergy, you can't go to Cambridge. The purpose of a university education is to help one work for the glory of God.'

'It can help one work for the glory of man, too, father,' said Angel. 'But I will do without [2] Cambridge.'

He went to London and became involved with a woman much older than himself who nearly trapped [3] him into marriage. Finally, disgusted with the city, he returned to the purity of the countryside and decided to learn all aspects of farming. So we find Angel Clare, at the age of twenty-six, learning how to milk cows in Talbothay's Dairy, renting a large attic room from Mr Crick, and eating his meals with the dairy workers.

At first he had chosen farming as a way of earning his living

1. **brightest** : (here) most intelligent.
2. **do without** : manage without something.
3. **trapped** : caught someone by a trick.

without giving up his intellectual freedom. Then gradually he came to love farm life. He liked the farm workers and took an interest in their characters and beliefs. He began to pay attention to the seasons and the changes of weather, morning and evening, night and noon, trees, mists, silences, and the voices of inanimate [1] things.

One morning, a few days after Tess's arrival at Talbothay's, Angel was sitting reading a book over his breakfast when he heard an unfamiliar voice. 'What a musical voice that is,' he thought. 'It must be the new milkmaid.'

'I don't know about ghosts, but I do know that our souls can leave our bodies when we are alive.'

'Really?' said Mr Crick, turning to Tess in surprise.

'If you lie on the grass at night and look straight up at the stars, you feel as if you are hundreds of miles away from your body.' Tess noticed that everyone, including Mr Clare, was listening to her. She blushed.

Clare continued to observe her. 'What a fresh and virginal [2] daughter of Nature!' he said to himself. He thought perhaps he had seen her somewhere before, but he could not remember where. But he began to think of Tess more than any of the other pretty milkmaids.

---

1. **inanimate** : not alive.
2. **virginal** : of a virgin, pure.

Go back to the text

1 **Answer the following questions.**

1. How was Tess affected by the coming of spring?
2. Why had Tess's attitude towards her ancestors changed?
3. How is Mr Crick considerate towards Tess? Use words from the text to show how.
4. Where had Tess previously seen Angel Clare?
5. How had Angel disappointed his father?
6. Why had Angel returned to the country from London?
7. How old was Angel?
8. What was Angel's attitude towards the farm workers? Use words/phrases from the text to support your view.
9. Why did Tess blush?
10. What was Angel's attitude towards Tess?

2 **Complete each space with the correct word from the text and then put the events into the correct sequence.**

1. Her experiences had changed her from a simple girl to a .... woman.
2. He liked the farm workers and .... an interest in their characters and beliefs.
3. On a beautiful morning in May, she took a .... cart to the town of Stourcastle.
4. Angel was the youngest and .... of the Reverend Clare's three sons.
5. Tess .... that everyone, including Mr Clare, was listening to her.
6. The dairy workers in the milk-house .... with interest as Tess approached.
7. Tess .... who the speaker was.

8. The fresh air and the .... of a new place made her cheeks pink and her eyes bright.

9. Clare continued to .... her.

10. Tess stayed with her family all .... the winter months.

Grammar

Relative Clauses

A **clause** is part of a sentence. A **relative clause** gives us more information about someone/something referred to in the **main clause** – the main part of the sentence.

1 Use **who** or **that** when you talk about people:
*A mechanic is someone **who/that** repairs cars.*

2 Use **which** or **that** when you talk about things:
*Barbara has a car, **which/that** she drives to work each day.*

3 Use **where** when you talk about places:
*The hotel **where** we stayed was excellent.*

4 Use **when** when you talk about a particular moment in time.
*Do you know the date **when** we have to take the exam?*

Defining and **non-defining** clauses.

a The information given in a **defining** relative clause is **essential** to the meaning of the sentence – it explains who or what we are talking about in the sentence.
*That is the man **who drove the car**.*

b The information given in a **non-defining** relative clause is extra information and **not essential** to the meaning of the sentence.
*The d'Urbervilles, **who were a noble family**, came from France.*

Punctuation is important in **non-defining** relative clauses. A **non-defining** relative clause is separated by the rest of the sentence by commas. In **defining relative clauses** there are **no** commas.

3 Read these sentences with relative clauses from the text. Decide if the clause is defining or non-defining. Insert commas where appropriate.

1. Her soul was that of a woman who had not been demoralised by her sorrows.
2. The cart passed by Kingsbere Church, where the d'Urbervilles were buried.
3. It is like a story from medieval times, when faith was a living thing.
4. He was the young gentleman who had not asked her to dance in the field at Marlott.
5. Tess went to bed in a large room over the milk-house, which she shared with three other milkmaids.
6. He went to London and became involved with a woman who nearly trapped him into marriage.
7. Angel was sitting reading a book when he heard an unfamiliar voice.

4 Using ideas from the text, join a sentence from box A with a sentence from box B. Use *which*, *when*, *where* or *who* in each case.

―――― A ――――

1. She heard of a dairy farm.
2. He returned to the countryside.
3. That young man is milking a cow.
4. Tess decided to go somewhere else.
5. Tess returned to her family.
6. Tess was milking the cow.

―――― B ――――

a   She stayed all through the winter.
b   She heard a voice ask, 'Why?'
c   No one knew her history.
d   The farm needed a milkmaid.
e   The man plays the harp.
f   He decided to learn all aspects of farming.

FCE 5 In Chapter Five Tess leaves Marlott. Many young people today also leave home. Write an article explaining why young people decide to leave home. Write between 120-180 words. You should write paragraphs about:

*   The advantages/disadvantages of living at home.

• The advantages/disadvantages of living alone or with friends.

The title of the article is *Mum, have you washed my shirt?* Present a balanced view which shows both sides of the argument. Your article will need an introduction and you should conclude with your personal view and opinion.

6 What kind of person is Angel? What do you think his name means? How would you compare Angel to Alec? Use evidence from the text to support your views. At the end of Chapter Five, Angel becomes interested in Tess. How do you think Tess will react?

Before you go on

1 In Chapter Six Tess and Angel become closer. However, Tess 'knew that she – with her terrible secret – could never marry anyone'. What does she mean? What do you think will happen between Tess and Angel? How do you think their relationship will end?

2 Listen to the first part of Chapter Six. For each question decide if the statement is true (T) or false (F).

	T	F
1. It was June and Tess was sitting in the garden.	☐	☐
2. Tess could hear Angel playing his guitar.	☐	☐
3. Angel couldn't play very well, but Tess was fascinated.	☐	☐
4. Tess sat down to listen in front of Angel.	☐	☐
5. The music was very moving and Tess became emotional.	☐	☐
6. When the music ended they talked about Angel's fears.	☐	☐

CHAPTER SIX

LOVE GROWS

One evening in June, as Tess was walking in the garden, she heard Angel playing his harp. Although he was not a very good player, Tess was fascinated. She followed the music, stepping softly through the wet grasses and weeds, sending mists of pollen [1] up into the air.

She stopped quite near to him, but he did not see her. The sounds of his harp passed through her like warm winds. Her body moved gently to the music, and her eyes filled with tears.

The tune ended, and Tess realised with alarm that he was walking towards her. She turned to go, but he called out to her, 'Why do you hurry away, Tess? Are you afraid?'

'Oh no, sir, not of outdoor things.'

'But you are afraid of indoor things?'

'Well – yes, sir.'

'What things?'

1.   **pollen** : fine, yellow powder formed in flowers.

'I can't say.'

'Life in general?'

'Yes, sir.'

'Ah – I am often afraid of that too. But why should a young girl like you feel that way?'

She was silent.

'Come, Tess, tell me. I promise I will tell no one else.'

'I seem to see a long line of tomorrows getting smaller and smaller in the distance. They all seem very cruel. They all seem to say, "I'm coming! Beware of me!"'

END

He was surprised that she had such sad imaginings. She seemed to be expressing, in her own simple way, the feelings of the age – the pain of modernism. What we call advanced ideas, he thought, are really just the latest definition of sensations [1] that men and women have been feeling for centuries. Still, it was strange that such ideas had come to her while she was still so young. It was more than strange: it was impressive, interesting, and pathetic. [2]

Tess thought it strange that a well-educated young gentleman could be afraid of life in general. Why did such an admirable poetic man not feel it a blessing to be alive? Certainly he was now working outside his social class, but he did so of his own free will. [3] Still, she wondered why such a book-loving, musical, thoughtful young man should decide to be a farmer and not a parson, like his father and brothers.

Every day, every hour, he learned one more little thing about her and she about him. At first she thought of him as an intellect rather than as a man. She compared her own modest world view

---

1. **sensations** : feelings.
2. **pathetic** : pitiful, sad.

3. **of his own free will** : without being forced.

to his and felt discouraged. One day, when he was talking about the ancient Greeks, he noticed that she looked sad.

'What's the matter, Tess?' he asked.

'I was just thinking about myself. My life has been wasted. [1] When I see how much you have read and seen and thought, I feel what a nothing I am!'

'Don't worry about that. I will help you learn anything you want to learn. I could teach you history, for example,' said Angel with enthusiasm.

'No.'

'Why not?'

'I don't want to learn that I am just one of many. I don't want to read books that tell me that my thoughts and actions are just like those of thousands of other people before me.'

'Don't you want to learn anything?'

'I want to know why the sun shines on the just and the unjust alike,' she answered in a trembling voice. 'But they don't teach that in books.'

'Don't be so bitter, Tess,' said Angel, although he had often felt the same way in the past. He looked at the side of her face and noticed the curl [2] of her eyelashes and the softness of her cheek. Reluctantly he went away.

When he was gone, Tess felt angry with herself. How stupid he must think her! She wanted him to like her. She thought about her noble ancestors. The next day, Tess asked Mr Crick if Mr Clare had respect for old noble families.

'Oh no!' replied Mr Crick emphatically. [3] 'Mr Clare is a rebel!

---

1. **wasted** : spent doing the wrong thing, used unnecessarily.

2. **curl** : (here) curve.

3. **emphatically** : clearly.

He hates old families. He says that they used up all their strength in the past and have nothing left now. He thinks that is why so many old families around here have lost their wealth and become common people. One of our dairymaids – Retty Priddle – is descended from the Paridelles, an old family that once owned lots of land around here. When Mr Clare found this out, he was very severe with the poor girl. "You'll never be a good milkmaid," he said, "because your family wasted all its strength fighting wars in the Middle Ages." And, some time ago, a boy came to ask for a job. He said his name was Matt. We asked him what his surname was, and he said he didn't have one. We asked him why, and he replied, "Well, I suppose my family has not been established long enough." When Mr Clare heard that, he jumped up and shook the boy's hand, saying, "You're exactly the kind of boy we want!"'

Tess was glad she had not told Angel about her family. Now she knew he did not respect old families. Besides, another dairymaid was as good as she in that respect. The story about the boy made Tess suspect that Angel was interested in her only because he thought that she too was from a new family.

The summer matured, producing a new generation of flowers, nightingales, and other ephemeral [1] creatures. The sunlight made flowers open and sap rise in the trees. The warmth of the sun filled the air with perfumes. Life at Talbothay's Dairy went on comfortably. Tess and Clare watched each other. They were balanced on the edge [2] of passion. They were moving irresistibly [3] towards each other, like two rivers in one valley.

1. **ephemeral** : lasting for a very short time.
2. **edge** : (here) limit or border.
3. **irresistibly** : in a way that cannot be resisted or that is so attractive that you cannot resist it.

Tess had never been so happy. One reason was that the life she lived now was completely appropriate for her. The other reason was that she, like Angel, was not yet aware of being in love. She was not yet at the stage when one asks oneself disturbing questions: Where will this new feeling carry me? What effect will it have on my future? What relation does it have to my past?

They met every day at dawn. It was Tess's job to wake the other dairy workers, and every morning she climbed the ladder to Angel's attic room and called him in a loud whisper. He rose immediately, got dressed, and went downstairs. All the other dairy workers slept for another fifteen minutes before rising. So usually Tess and Angel spent the first fifteen minutes of the day together, alone, out in the humid air and the rosy light of dawn. Sometimes it seemed to them that they were Adam and Eve, alone on the earth.

The soft light of those mornings often reminded him of the Resurrection [1] hour, though he never imagined that the Magdalen [2] was by his side. The early-morning light gave her face a radiant quality, so that she looked ghostly, like a soul walking free of its body. It was then she impressed him most deeply. She was no longer a milkmaid: she seemed to him the essence of womanhood. He called her Artemis [3] and Demeter. [4] She did not like this, because she did not understand the references. 'Call me Tess,' she said, and he did.

One evening, Tess went to bed early. She fell asleep, but a little later she was woken by the sounds of the other three milkmaids who shared her room. She opened her eyes and saw

1. **the Resurrection** : the rising of Jesus from the tomb.
2. **Magdalen** : an Italian nun who is given the title 'saint' by the church after she died; (here) a symbol of Tess.
3. **Artemis** : virgin goddess of hunting, who helped women in childbirth.
4. **Demeter** : goddess of agriculture.

them looking out of the window together, watching someone in the garden below.

'Don't push! You can see as well as I can,' said Retty, the youngest of the three.

'It's useless for you or me to be in love with him,' said Marian, the eldest. 'He loves someone else.'

'Izz loves him too,' said Retty. 'I saw her kissing his shadow on the milk-house wall.'

Izz blushed. 'Well, I do love him, but so do you, and so does Marian.'

Marian's round face was always very pink; now it became even pinker. 'But he likes Tess best,' she said. 'I've seen him watching her.'

'He won't marry any of us,' said Izz. 'He is a gentleman, and we are just milkmaids.'

Tess lay in her bed and thought about Angel. One day she had heard Mr Crick joking with him. Mr Crick had said, 'You will marry a fine lady, sir!' But Angel had replied, 'No, I won't. Perhaps I will marry a farm-woman – someone who can help me on the farm.' But Tess knew that she – with her terrible secret – could never marry anyone now.

From that day on, Tess tried to avoid Angel's company. When she was with him, she drew his attention to [1] the other milkmaids.

'They blush when you look at them,' she said. 'Why don't you marry one of them?' She felt that this was the right thing to do. What right had she – who could not marry anyone – to enjoy the sunshine of his smiles? Now that she knew the other milkmaids

1. **drew his attention to** : (here) made him become interested in other milkmaids.

loved him, she felt it was her duty to give them a chance of winning his love. Nevertheless, it broke her heart to do so.

The hot weather of July came, then the rains began. It rained heavily and frequently. The fields were wet, and the streams [1] were full.

One Sunday morning, after the milking was done, Tess and the other three milkmaids decided to go to Mellstock Church. It had rained heavily the night before, but now the sun was shining. Walking along the lane to Mellstock, the girls came to a place where the rain had flooded [2] the road. On weekdays, they simply walked through the water, but today they were wearing their best shoes.

Suddenly they saw Angel Clare walking towards them through the water.

'Are you trying to get to the church?' he asked. 'If you want, I will carry you over.'

The four girls blushed.

'You can't carry me, sir. I'm too heavy,' said Marian.

'Nonsense!' said Angel. 'Put your arms around my shoulders. That's right! Now off we go!'

He walked back across the flood with Marian in his arms, then returned to the other three. One by one, he carried the blushing milkmaids across the water. He left Tess till last.

'You must be so tired, Mr Clare. Perhaps I can walk around the flood.'

'No, Tess,' he replied. 'I carried the others just so that I could have the pleasure of carrying you.'

---

1. **streams** : small, narrow rivers.
2. **flooded** : covered.

'They are better women than I.'

'Not to me,' he replied.

She blushed at this.

No definite words of love had been spoken, and he did not wish to take unfair advantage of the situation. He walked slowly, however, enjoying every moment that she was in his arms. At last they reached the other side, and he set her down. He said goodbye and went on towards Talbothay's.

The four milkmaids moved on together as before, but the mood was changed. Finally Marian broke the silence. 'He likes you best!' she said to Tess. 'We could see it as he brought you over.'

Tess's heart ached. She knew she loved him. She had tried to repress [1] her feelings to give one of her friends a chance of winning his love. But she had not tried hard enough, and this was the result.

That night, in the bedroom, Tess said, 'I don't think that marrying is in his mind at all. But if he asks me, I will refuse. I will refuse any man who asks me.'

'Why?' asked Retty.

'It cannot be!' said Tess.

'I heard that his family has chosen a wife for him,' said Izz. 'She is a lady. They say he does not love her, but he is sure to marry her.'

'Ah!' thought Tess. 'So it was just a passing summer love, after all!'

---

1. **repress** : stop.

Go back to the text

FCE 1 For each question below, choose the correct answer A, B, C or D.

1. Tess was fascinated when Angel played the harp
   ☐ **A** even if she didn't understand music.
   ☐ **B** even if the music made her sad.
   ☐ **C** even though he wasn't very good.
   ☐ **D** even though the music made her feel cold.

2. As the tune ended Tess turned to go because
   ☐ **A** she was afraid of Angel.
   ☐ **B** she didn't like the outdoors.
   ☐ **C** she preferred to be indoors.
   ☐ **D** she was still upset about her past experiences.

3. At first Tess thought Angel was
   ☐ **A** physically attractive.
   ☐ **B** an intellectual.
   ☐ **C** only a parson's son.
   ☐ **D** a poet.

4. Angel disliked old families because
   ☐ **A** they had too much money.
   ☐ **B** they were strong and powerful.
   ☐ **C** he felt they had nothing to offer.
   ☐ **D** in his opinion they were vulgar.

5. Tess thought Angel was interested in her because
   ☐ **A** she came from an old family.
   ☐ **B** he respected her.
   ☐ **C** she was a good milkmaid.
   ☐ **D** he believed she came from an ordinary family.

6. Tess woke Angel each morning because

☐ **A** she was in love with him.

☐ **B** it was her job.

☐ **C** he asked her to.

☐ **D** he had trouble waking up.

7. Why did Tess start to avoid Angel?

☐ **A** She felt her past would create problems.

☐ **B** He was going to marry a fine lady.

☐ **C** He loved one of the other milkmaids.

☐ **D** The other girls were jealous of her.

8. Angel carried the milkmaids across the water because

☐ **A** the area was flooded.

☐ **B** the girls were wearing their best shoes.

☐ **C** they were going to church.

☐ **D** he wanted an excuse to carry Tess.

9. Tess's heart ached because

☐ **A** Angel didn't share her feelings.

☐ **B** the milkmaids were angry with her.

☐ **C** she was in love with Angel.

☐ **D** she hadn't discouraged Angel enough.

10. Tess felt that Angel's feelings towards her were not serious because

☐ **A** Angel was attracted to Retty.

☐ **B** his wife had already been chosen.

☐ **C** Angel didn't love her.

☐ **D** the summer would soon be over.

2 Look at the adjectives in the box. Using the text to help, which of them would you use to describe Tess, Angel and Alec? Use a maximum of three adjectives for each of the characters.

artistic	bitter	clever	confused	deceitful	gentle
guilty	handsome	hard-working	naive	uncaring	
quick-tempered	rebellious	reckless	romantic	shy	

Alec	Tess	Angel

3 Explain your choice of adjectives. Use extracts and events from the text to support your choice.

4 Choose adjectives from Activity 2 to complete the sentences below.

1. Angel knew a lot about history. He was very ....

2. Tess was very .... She believed what people told her.

3. With his dark skin and nice smile, Alec was considered to be a .... man.

4. Because of what happened to her in the woods, Tess felt ....

5. Alec was very .... when he said he had ridden into the woods because it was a lovely night.

6. Angel didn't want to marry the girl his parents had chosen for him. He was very ....

Grammar

Conditional Sentences: types 0, 1 and 2 – Revision

Consider how these three conditional sentences are different. Then match each type with the three different situations below.

1 *If I get up early, I go swimming.*   (type 0)
   If + present verb, **present.**

2 *If I get up early, I will go swimming.*   (type 1)
   If + present, will future.

3 *If I got up in time, I'd go swimming.*   (type 2)
   If + past verb, **would** + verb.

A an **imaginary** situation

B a general rule that is **always true**

C a **possible** future situation

---

5 Match a clause from box A with a clause from box B to make conditional sentences. In each case indicate what type of conditional sentence it is.

——— A ———
1. If you tell me,
2. If you want to learn,
3. If Tess was from an old family,
4. If it is warm,
5. If Angel called her Artemis,
6. If he asks me to marry him,
7. If it's Sunday,
8. If she repressed her true feelings,

——— B ———
A the air is filled with the perfume of flowers.
B maybe one of the others would win his love.
C she wouldn't like it.
D I will help you.
E perhaps Angel wouldn't be interested in her.
F they go to church.
G I promise I will tell no one else.
H I will refuse.

T: GRADE **8**

6 Choose a section of Chapter Six. Think about the following questions.

A What happens in this section of Chapter Six you have chosen? Give a brief account of the section.

B Why did you choose this section? What does it show about the relationship between Angel and Tess?

C What does it show us about the characters of Angel and Tess?

 7 Describe someone close to you. This could be a member of your family, a good friend or a boy/girlfriend. Try to use some of the adjectives from Activity 2 to describe the person. Use between 120-180 words. Organise your description using the following paragraph plan.

Paragraph 1

Begin with the name of the person. Say how long you have known them. Say when and how you first met and describe the situation.

Paragraph 2

Physical description – main features, face, build and height. Describe a situation which illustrates your friend's character. Description of character – positive and negative sides. Which character is your friend similar to in *Tess of the d'Urbervilles*?

Paragraph 3

Think back to when you first met. Consider your first impressions. Have these changed since that first meeting? Conclude by saying why this person is important to you.

NO SEX, PLEASE, WE'RE VICTORIANS!

It is difficult for us to imagine how sensitive and censorious [1] the Victorians were about sexual matters or their representation in the arts. These were the people who painted drapery [2] over the nudes of the great masters. They read Shakespeare in a censored edition – Thomas Bowdler's *Family Shakespeare* – in which all sexual references had been deleted. Most Victorian ladies went to their marriage beds without knowing anything about sex. At the same time, there were 80,000 prostitutes working in London alone. A Victorian woman who was known to have had sex before marriage 'lost her reputation', was considered 'a fallen woman', was ostracised, [3] and had no chance of marrying. At the same time, the American poet Ralph Waldo Emerson was shocked to hear Charles Dickens say that he only knew two or three Englishmen who were virgins when they married. A similar double standard existed in reading matter. A novel in English was banned if it contained any description of sex. But the works of Sophocles, Sappho, Homer, and Ovid, which contain explicit [4] treatments of sex, including adultery, rape, homosexuality, and incest, [5] were available in the original Greek and Latin to thirteen-year-old, ruling-class, English school boys. This double standard made life extremely difficult for novelists. The novel-reading public was largely female. Victorian men did not want their wives and daughters to read anything about sex, so English novels approached the subject at their peril. [6] The publishing history of *Tess of the d'Urbervilles* is a prime example of this. Hardy began

1. **censorious** : severely critical.
2. **drapery** : cloths.
3. **ostracised** : excluded from a group.
4. **explicit** : clear and open.
5. **incest** : sexual intercourse between people who are too closely related to marry.
6. **peril** : risk.

writing *Tess* in 1888. He had an agreement for publication in instalments with a newspaper syndicate.[1] However, when they discovered that Tess has an illegitimate baby in the novel, the publishers broke the contract. Two magazines refused to publish *Tess* for the same reason. *The Graphic* magazine agreed to publish if Hardy cut out the offensive material, and Hardy reluctantly did so. The dance at Chaseborough had to go, as did the life and death of Tess's illegitimate baby. Angel could not carry the milkmaids across the flooded road. Tess and Alec had to have separate rooms at the hotel in Sandbourne. This expurgated[2] version of *Tess* was published in instalments in *The Graphic* between July and December of 1891. When the novel was published in book form in December 1891, however, it was in Hardy's original version. The reviewers were outraged. *The Saturday Review* wrote, 'Mr Hardy... tells an unpleasant story in a very unpleasant way'. A review in *The Nation* described Tess as 'a weak and sensual[3] woman' and saw Angel Clare as 'the only moral character in the novel'. In his notebook Hardy wrote an exasperated[4] reaction to these reviews: 'Well, if this sort of thing continues, no more novel writing for me. A man must be a fool to stand up to be shot at.' After *Tess*, Hardy wrote one more novel. *Jude the Obscure* appeared in 1895 – the year Oscar Wilde was condemned and imprisoned for homosexuality. The reviews of *Jude* were as censorious of those of *Tess* had been, and Hardy – sick of the prudery[5] and hypocrisy[6] of his fellow-Victorians – stopped writing fiction.

1. **syndicate** : group of business companies combined to undertake a joint project.
2. **expurgated** : with improper parts removed from a book.
3. **sensual** : enjoying physical pleasure.
4. **exasperated** : very angry.
5. **prudery** : the quality of being easily shocked.
6. **hypocrisy** : insincerity.

Stamp
Here

BLACK CAT ENGLISH CLUB
The Commercial Press (Hong Kong) Ltd.
9/F, Eastern Central Plaza,
3 Yiu Hing Road, Shau Kei Wan,
Hong Kong

BLACK CAT ENGLISH CLUB
Membership Application Form

BLACK CAT ENGLISH CLUB is for those who love English reading and seek for better English to share and learn with fun together.

Benefits offered:
- *Membership Card*
- *Book discount coupon*
- *English learning e-forum*
- *English learning activities*
- *Black Cat English Reward Scheme*
- *Surprise gift and more...*

Simply fill out the application form below and fax it back to 2565 1113 or send it back to the address at the back.

Join Now! It's FREE exclusively for readers who have purchased *Black Cat English Readers* !

(Please fill out the form with **BLOCK LETTERS**.)

The title of Black Cat English Reader/book set that you have purchased: _____

English Name: _____ (Surname) _____ (Given Name)

Chinese Name: _____

Address:

Tel: _____ Fax: _____

Email: _____

(Login password for e-forum will be sent to this email address.)

Sex: ❏ Male ❏ Female

Education Background: ❏ Primary 1-3 ❏ Primary 4-6 ❏ Junior Secondary Education (F1-3) ❏ Senior Secondary Education (F4-5) ❏ Matriculation ❏ College ❏ University or above

Age: ❏ 6 - 9 ❏ 10 - 12 ❏ 13 - 15 ❏ 16 - 18 ❏ 19 - 24 ❏ 25 - 34 ❏ 35 - 44 ❏ 45 - 54 ❏ 55 or above

Occupation: ❏ Student ❏ Teacher ❏ White Collar ❏ Blue Collar ❏ Professional ❏ Manager ❏ Business Owner ❏ Housewife ❏ Others (please specify: _____)

As a member, what would you like **BLACK CAT ENGLISH CLUB** to offer:

❏ Member gathering/ party ❏ English class with native teacher ❏ English competition
❏ Newsletter ❏ Online sharing ❏ Book fair
❏ Book discount ❏ Others (please specify: _____)

Other suggestions to **BLACK CAT ENGLISH CLUB**: _____

_____

Please sign here: _____ (Date: _____)

Visit us at Quality English Learning Online http://publish.commercialpress.com.hk/qel

1 Find words or phrases in the dossier on Victorian values that mean the following:

1. A noun used to talk about very good painters.
2. An adjective used to describe something which has been changed for reasons of morality or good taste.
3. A verb used to talk about removing something.
4. An adjective used to describe someone excluded from a group.
5. An adjective used to describe something prohibited or forbidden.
6. An adjective used to describe something very clearly detailed or expressed.
7. A noun used to talk about parts or portions of something.
8. An adjective used to describe a baby born to an unmarried couple.
9. An adjective used to describe something contrary to established values.
10. An adjective used to describe a text or book removed of its offensive parts.
11. A verb used to express strong disapproval.
12. A noun used to talk about having beliefs contrary to one's actual behaviour.

2 On page 90 there is a reference to 'double standards'. In the article, underline two examples of double standards. Can you think of any double standards that exist between men and women today? Think about the following questions:

- Which statement do you agree with: 'Men and Women are the same' or 'Men and Women are different but should respect each other', and explain why?
- In what way are women still discriminated against?
- Are there any ways in which men are discriminated against?

Before you go on

T: GRADE 8

1 Topic – The supernatural

In Chapter Seven a cock, a type of bird, crows three times while pointing straight at Angel. This is considered very unlucky. What are the superstitions in your country? Choose an object, or photo which is linked to a superstition. Think about the following questions.

A   Can you describe your superstition? Does it bring good luck or bad luck?

B   What are the origins of your superstition?

C   Do you believe in this superstition or superstitions in general? Why/Why not?

 2 You will hear the first part of Chapter Seven. For each question, decide which character would make the following statements.

A   Tess

B   Angel

1.   ☐ It's so hot I can't do anything.

2.   ☐ I'll go to the corner of the field to be on my own.

3.   ☐ I'll pretend to milk this cow and watch what is happening.

4.   ☐ This scene is so beautiful it looks like a picture.

5.   ☐ To milk these cows I have to move my hands all the time.

6.   ☐ This scene is so beautiful it could be the subject of a poem.

CHAPTER SEVEN

The Consequence

ugust was hot. At midday the landscape seemed paralysed [1] by the heat. Angel found the heat oppressive, but he was even more troubled by his growing passion for the soft and silent Tess.

Now they milked the cows in the fields, for coolness and convenience. One afternoon, at milking-time, Angel found Tess in a secluded [2] corner of the field, milking one of the cows. He placed his stool beside a nearby cow and sat down. But he did not start milking. Instead he watched Tess. She was leaning her cheek against the flank [3] of the cow. Her face in profile [4] was like a delicate cameo [5] against the brown background of the cow. Her eyes gazed dreamily off to the horizon. The picture was still,

1. **paralysed** : losing ability to move, act.
2. **secluded** : hidden, distant.
3. **flank** : side.
4. **in profile** : seen from the side.
5. **cameo** : small piece of hard stone with a raised design.

except for Tess's hands, which moved gently and rhythmically, like the beating of a heart.

How lovable her face was to him. It was full of vitality and warmth. He loved her eloquent [1] eyes, her fair skin, her arched brows, [2] and the beautiful shape of her chin and throat. Above all he loved her mouth. It reminded him of that image in Elizabethan poetry of the beloved's lips and teeth like roses filled with snow. He was tempted to call Tess's mouth perfect, but no, it was not perfect. And that touch of imperfection gave it sweetness and humanity.

END

Overcome with emotion, Angel leapt up and knelt beside her. He put his arms around her. She was surprised, but, when she saw it was he, she yielded to [3] his embrace with a cry of pleasure.

'Forgive me, Tess dear!' he whispered. 'I should have asked. I love you!'

Tess's eyes filled with tears.

Just then they heard Mr Crick approaching. They went back to their milking as if nothing had happened. But something had happened. The universe had changed for Angel and Tess.

Angel's embrace had been impulsive. Afterwards he was amazed and frightened by what he had done. But now it was clear to him that she loved him. Why should he not marry her?

The next day he went to Emminster to discuss it with his family. His parents were not enthusiastic about him marrying a milkmaid. They wanted him to marry Mercy Chant, the daughter of a neighbouring clergyman.

1. **eloquent** : expressive, good at speaking.
2. **arched brows** : curved eye brows.
3. **yielded to** : accepted.

'Ah, well!' said the Reverend Clare finally. 'I suppose a farmwoman will be a better wife for you than a fine lady. And I am glad to hear you say that she is a good Christian.'

Angel got back to Talbothay's at three o'clock. The dairy workers were taking their afternoon nap. [1] The first to wake up was Tess. She descended the stairs, yawning, [2] and Angel saw the red interior of her mouth, like a snake's. When she saw him she was startled: 'O Mr Clare! You frightened me !'

Angel put his arms around her. 'Darling Tessy!' he whispered. 'Don't call me Mister any more. I have hurried back from Emminster to ask you something very important. Will you be my wife?'

Tess went pale. 'No – I cannot,' she murmured.

'Don't you love me?'

'O yes!'

'Then why won't you marry me?'

Tess was forced to invent a reason: 'Your family won't like it. I am just a milkmaid.'

'But that is why I went home, Tessy. I told them about you, and they have agreed to our marriage.'

'But I cannot agree!'

'Was it too sudden, Tessy? Do you need time to think about it?'

'Yes,' she said, relieved.

So Angel did not ask again for a few days. A terrible struggle was going on in Tess's heart. She knew that, as an honourable woman, she must refuse him. But she wanted so much to accept

---

1. **nap** : short sleep.
2. **yawning** : opening and closing mouth because she was tired.

him! The other milkmaids noticed her distress [1] and guessed that something important had happened.

On Sunday he asked her again, and again she refused. 'One day she will accept me,' thought Angel with confidence. Therefore he was patient and loving.

Days and weeks went by. September came and went. Occasionally Angel asked his question again. She tried, on one or two occasions, to tell him her terrible secret, but she failed. She was afraid of losing his love.

One day Angel volunteered to drive the milk to the station. He asked Tess to accompany him, and she accepted.

'Tess,' he said, as they drove along. 'You must tell me why you refuse to marry me.'

'It is for your own good,' Tess replied. 'It is to do with my past.'

'Tell me.'

'Well, a few years ago,' Tess began, 'my family was in trouble. We were very poor, and my father drank a little –'

'That's not unusual,' said Angel.

'But there was something unusual. Our family is descended from the d'Urbervilles – '

'Really? Is that all? Is that the reason you refuse me?' Angel laughed and stopped the cart.

Poor Tess did not have the strength to tell the rest of her story. 'Yes,' she said. 'Mr Crick told me that you hated old families.'

'Well, it's true that I hate the privileges [2] of aristocracy, but that makes no difference to us. Now, will you marry me?'

---

1. **distress** : (here) great confusion.
2. **privileges** : special rights or advantages.

'Yes!' cried Tess, and she burst into tears.

Angel was surprised. There was nothing hysterical [1] in Tess's nature. 'Why are you crying, dearest?' he asked.

'O I wish I had never been born!' said the poor girl.

'Tess! Don't you love me? Why are you so sad?'

'Of course I love you,' Tess replied. She put her arms around his neck and, for the first time, Angel tasted the kisses of an impassioned [2] woman who loved him with all her heart and soul.

The next day Tess wrote a letter to her mother, asking her advice. Joan wrote back immediately, saying that Tess should never tell Angel about her past troubles. Tess realised that her mother's views of life were superficial. But she thought her advice was sound. [3]

'Tess has agreed to marry me!' said Angel to the people at Talbothay's the next day. 'We will buy our own farm in the English Midlands and be married in December.'

Tess watched the other milkmaids nervously. 'Now they will hate me!' she thought. But that night, in their bedroom, Retty, Izz, and Marian all crowded round her. They embraced and kissed her, looking at her in wonder, [4] amazed that a simple milkmaid was going to be his wife. Tess was moved by their goodness. That night she wept silently. 'I will tell Angel my secret after all!' she thought. 'He is so good, and they are so good. I must be good too!'

Tess adored Angel. Sometimes he caught her gazing at him with eyes full of love. They spent all their free time together now. Throughout the month of October, they went for walks in the

1. **hysterical** : wild, unreasonable.
2. **impassioned** : showing strong deep feeling.
3. **sound** : good, reliable, correct.
4. **wonder** : great surprise.

afternoons. In the autumn sunshine, they walked by the river and planned their future.

In November, however, Angel changed his plans. During a visit to the Wellbridge flourmill, he decided to spend some time there after leaving Talbothay's. There he could learn all about the milling of flour, but that was not the reason he decided to go. He made the decision when he discovered that the farmhouse there was an old mansion that once belonged to the d'Urbervilles. Angel thought it was the perfect place for their honeymoon.

One day they went into the village to do some Christmas shopping. Tess waited outside the inn, while Angel went to get the horse and gig. Two men came out of the inn while Tess was waiting.

'What a pretty maid!' said one.

'Yes,' said the other, looking at her closely. She thought he was a Trantridge man. 'She is pretty. But, unless I am mistaken...'

Tess did not hear the rest of what he said, but Angel did. He was coming back from the stables and passed the man as he spoke. The insult infuriated [1] Angel. He struck the man on the chin.

'I made a mistake,' said the man. 'I thought she was another woman.'

As the wedding day approached, Tess thought about her confession. 'O, when and how can I tell him?' she asked herself again and again. One night she heard a noise in Angel's room. She went to see what was the matter.

'I'm sorry I woke you, Tess,' said Angel. 'I dreamt I was fighting with that man again.' The noise you heard was me hitting the bed. I sometimes do strange things like that in my sleep.' Now Tess felt that she must confess everything to Angel. She decided to write him a letter.

---

1. **infuriated** : made someone extremely angry.

On the evening before the wedding, Tess wrote the letter, explaining all her past sorrows. She crept [1] up the attic stairs and put the letter under Angel's door.

The next morning, he greeted her with his usual warmth and affection. 'He can't have read my letter,' thought Tess, and she ran up the attic stairs to his room. The letter was still there. Tess had pushed it under the door, but it had gone under the carpet. Angel had not seen it. He still knew nothing of her past.

That day was full of preparations for the wedding. She tried to talk to him when they met on the stairs, knowing it was her last chance to confess before their marriage. 'Don't worry, my dear,' Angel said 'We will tell each other all our faults this evening, after the wedding, when we are alone together.'

And so they were married. They left the church in a coach that Angel had rented. As Tess approached it, she said, 'I've seen this coach somewhere before.'

'Perhaps you have heard the legend of the d'Urberville coach,' said Angel, 'and this one reminds you of it.'

'No. I haven't heard. Tell me.'

'Well – a d'Urberville of the sixteenth century committed a terrible crime in the family coach. Ever since, members of the family see the coach whenever – but let's not think of sad things.'

'Do we see the coach when we are going to die or when we have committed a crime?'

'Never mind,' said Angel, silencing [2] her with a kiss.

Back at the dairy, Tess went up to her old bedroom to change her clothes. She knelt down and tried to pray to God, but instead she prayed to Angel: 'O my dear! The woman you love is not my

1. **crept** : (here) moved slowly and carefully.
2. **silencing** : causing someone to be quiet.

real self but the woman I might have been!'

When the time came to leave Talbothay's, Mr Crick and the dairy workers came out to wave goodbye to them as they drove off. The three milkmaids watched sadly as Tess and Angel got onto the gig. Then a cock crew. [1]

'A cock crowing in the afternoon!' exclaimed Mr Crick.

'That's bad,' said one of the dairymen.

The cock crew again, pointing its beak straight at Clare.

'I don't want to hear it. Drive on,' said Tess to her husband.

He drove away, and everyone called out 'Goodbye! Goodbye!'

Then the cock crew again.

Mr Crick turned towards the bird, crying, 'Stop that noise!'

'It only means that the weather is changing,' said a milkmaid. 'Not what you think: that's impossible!' [2]

'Welcome to your ancestral mansion!' said Angel, when they arrived at the house in Wellbridge. There was no one there except a servant. 'The farmer who lives here has gone to visit friends,' Angel told Tess. 'So, for the first few days, we will have the entire house to ourselves.' [3]

The servant led them upstairs. Tess was startled by two large portraits hanging on the wall. 'What horrible women!' she cried. One of the women had a long pointed face. The expression in her eyes suggested cruel treachery. [4] The other had large teeth and an arrogant expression.

'Who are the women in those portraits?' said Angel.

1. **cock crew** : A cock is a male chicken. The noise cocks make is called 'crowing'. The past tense of 'crow' is 'crew'.
2. **Not... impossible** : a cock crew three times when Peter denied that he knew Jesus, thus the cock crow is a symbol of betrayal.
3. **will... to ourselves** : (here) we will be alone in the house.
4. **treachery** : betrayal.

'Ladies of the d'Urberville family,' the servant replied.

Angel noticed that, despite their unpleasant features and expressions, these women resembled Tess. He regretted that he had chosen this house for their honeymoon.

They washed their hands in the same basin. 'Which are your fingers, and which are mine?' asked Angel playfully.

'They are all yours,' Tess replied.

'How sweet she is!' he thought. 'And now she depends on me entirely for her happiness. I will never neglect her or hurt her!'

The servant prepared their supper and then went home. The sun set, and the wind made strange noises outside the house. It began to rain.

'That cock knew that the weather was changing,' said Angel.

He saw that Tess was still anxious and sad, so he took a package out of his pocket. 'Look, Tess. My father sent a wedding present for you.' He handed her the package. Tess opened it and found a necklace, bracelets, and earrings. She was afraid to touch them at first, but her eyes sparkled. [1] 'Are they mine?' she asked.

'Yes. When my godmother died, she left these jewels for my wife. Put them on.' When Tess was wearing the jewels, Angel stepped back to look at her. 'How beautiful you are!'

Just then there was a knock at the door. Angel went downstairs and let in the man who had brought their luggage from Talbothay's. 'You're late, Jonathan,' said Angel.

'Well, terrible things have been happening at the Dairy since you and your wife left this afternoon. Retty Priddle tried to kill herself. She threw herself in the pond and nearly drowned. [2]

---

1. **sparkled** : lit up with excitement.
2. **drowned** : died underwater without being able to breathe.

Fortunately, two men passing by jumped in to save her. And Marian came home completely drunk, although she never usually drinks much.'

Tess went pale. They were innocent girls who had experienced the unhappiness of unrequited love. [1] They had deserved a happier fate. She – who deserved [2] to be unhappy – was the chosen one. It was wicked of her to take all without paying. 'I will pay now,' she thought. 'I will tell him everything.'

When Jonathan had gone, they sat by the fire, holding hands.

'I want to make a confession,' said Angel suddenly.

To Tess, his desire to confess seemed like a gift from God. How strange it was! He seemed to be her double. [3]

'I didn't tell you earlier, because I was afraid of losing you,' he began. He told her of his time in London and his relationship with the older woman. When he had finished, he asked, 'Do you forgive me?'

'O Angel! I am almost glad – because now you can forgive me!'

'Oh yes. Now let me hear your little confession,' he said, smiling.

'It is as serious as yours, perhaps even more so.'

'It can't be more serious, dearest.'

'No, it can't!' cried Tess joyfully, 'because it is the same!'

She bent forward by the fire, and her shadow was large on the wall behind her. The light from the fire glittered in her jewels. Each diamond seemed to give a sinister [4] wink. [5] She told him the whole story of her acquaintance with Alec d'Urberville and its results, speaking softly but without hesitation.

1. **unrequited love** : loving someone who does not love you.
2. **deserved** : merited.
3. **double** : person that looks very like another.
4. **sinister** : suggesting evil.
5. **wink** : close one eye to suggest secret knowledge.

Go back to the text

1 Decide if the following statements are true (T) or false (F).

	T	F
1. Angel had planned to embrace Tess.	☐	☐
2. Angel's parents approved of the marriage.	☐	☐
3. Tess accepted the first time Angel asked her to marry him.	☐	☐
4. Driving to the milk station, Tess told Angel all about her past.	☐	☐
5. Joan advised Tess not to tell Angel what had happened with Alec.	☐	☐
6. On hearing that Tess and Angel were to marry, the other milk maids were jealous.	☐	☐
7. Angel regretted choosing the old mansion for the honeymoon.	☐	☐
8. Angel bought Tess some jewellery as a wedding present.	☐	☐
9. Retty drowned herself in the pond with two men.	☐	☐
10. Tess was happy to hear Angel's confession.	☐	☐

Grammar

Modal Verbs

Modal verbs are auxiliary verbs. They are used to give meaning to the main verb.

Use **must/have to** when it is **necessary** to do something.
*We **must** leave now.*
*We **have to** leave now.*

Use **must** to talk about the **present** or **future**.
*We **must** go **today/tomorrow**.*
*You **mustn't** walk on the grass.*

Use **have to** to talk about the **past, present** or **future**.
*We **had to** go **yesterday**.*
*We **have to** go today.*
*We **will have to** go tomorrow.*

Note: **Must** and **have to** are **both** used to express **strong obligations**.
Must is often used to express the **internal motivation** of the **speaker**.
Have to is often used to express the **external motivation** from **a third person**.
*I **must** clean my teeth.* (the **speaker** thinks it's a good idea – *internal*)
*I **have** to pay taxes.* (the **government** thinks it's a good idea – *external*)

Use **should** to give an **opinion** or **advice**.
*You seem tired. You **should** go to bed.*
*You **shouldn't** smoke so much.*
*She **should** apologise for what she said.* (it's a good idea.)
*She **must** apologise.* (she has no alternative)

2 For each question, complete the second sentence. Your opinion on the situation is in brackets. Use *should* in each case and the number of words indicated.

0. Parson Tringham told Jack about his ancestors. (You think it was a bad idea).
I don't think the parson *should have told* Jack about his past.
(3 words)

1. Angel's parents want him to marry Mercy Chant. (You think it's a bad idea.)
I .... marry Mercy Chant. (4 words)

2. Tess is upset about her past. (You think it's better to say something to Angel.)
I .... about her past. (5 words)

3. Overcome with emotion, Angel suddenly embraced Tess. (You think it's a bad idea.)
Angel .... Tess. (4 words)

4. Angel's family agreed to the marriage. (You think it's a bad idea.)
I don't .... to the marriage. (5 words)

3 Complete the sentences below. Use *must* or *have to* in each case and the number of words indicated.

0. 'Father,' said Tess, 'you *have to drive* the goods to town tomorrow.' (3 words)

1. 'I .... Angel my terrible secret,' said Tess. (2 words)

2. 'You .... again. I can't marry you,' Tess told Angel. (3 words)

3. Tess decided that she .... a letter to Angel. (3 words)

4. 'I .... everything to Tess,' said Angel, 'she deserves it.' (4 words)

4 Complete the sentences below. In each case decide if the obligation is internal or external. If the obligation is internal, use *must*. If the obligation is external, use *have to*.

1. You .... pay taxes. It's the law.

2. If I want to pass the exam, I .... study more.

3. I'm feeling really tired. I .... get some sleep.

4. My mother said I .... stay in tonight.

5. Before you can drive a car you .... pass a driving test.

6. I'm not feeling very well. I .... go to the doctor's.

5 Match a clause from box A with a clause from box B. Use *should* or *must* in each case.

———— A ————	———— B ————
1. She knew that as an honourable woman she	**A** why you refuse to marry him.
2. Joan wrote back saying that Tess	**B** have asked.
3. 'Forgive me, Tess dear,' he whispered, 'I...'	**C** refuse him.
4. Tell Angel	**D** never tell Angel about her past.

6 In this chapter Joan advises Tess not to tell Angel anything about her past. Think about the following questions:

- Do you think Joan's advice was good advice?
- Do you ever tell lies? In what situations would you tell a lie?
- What is worse, telling a lie, or saying nothing? Think of example situations.

7 An 'Agony Aunt' works for a newspaper or magazine. Readers write with their problems. The job of the 'Agony Aunt' is to reply offering advice. Imagine Angel has written to a modern magazine. Reply to him using *should* and *must* where possible. In your reply, consider the following points:

- Angel and Tess both had previous relationships.
- Tess accepted Angel's secret.
- Angel's shock at Tess's secret.
- Outline the similarities/differences between the two previous relationships.
- The future and what Angel should/must do.

Write your letter in 120-180 words. Begin like this:

Dear Angel,

I was really sorry to hear about your sad wedding night. In my opinion...

Before you go on

 1 Read the beginning of Chapter Eight below. Some of the lines are correct, and some have a word which should not be there. If a line is correct, put a tick (✓) at the end of the line. If a line has a word which should not be there, write the word at the end of the line. There are two examples (0 and 00) at the beginning. Then read Chapter Eight to check your answers.

0.	Her narrative ended. She had not tried out to excuse	*...out...*
00.	herself, and she had not wept. The fire seemed like a	...✓...
1.	demon, laughing at her fate. Angel who stood up and	....
2.	began walking around the room. His face was pale and	....
3.	haggard. 'Why not didn't you tell me this before?' he	....
4.	asked. 'Ah! Now I remember it. You tried, but I	....
5.	interrupted you.' 'In the name of our love, forgive me!'	....
6.	she whispered with a dry mouth. 'I have forgiven of you	....
7.	for the same. Forgive me as you are forgiven. *I* forgive	....
8.	*you*, Angel.' 'Yes, you do.' 'But you do not forgive me?' 'O	....
9.	Tess, forgiveness does not apply to this case! You were	....
10.	one person and then now you are another.' He began to	....
11.	laugh out. It was as unnatural and horrible as a laugh in	....
12.	hell. 'O stop!' cried Tess. 'Forgive me! I thought that you	....
13.	loved me, my very self! I love you, and my love will	....
14.	never change. How much can you stop loving me?' 'The	....
15.	woman I have been loving is not you too.' Tess burst into	....
16.	a flood of self-pitying tears. He waited patiently and	....
17.	apathetically until she stopped crying.	....

CHAPTER EIGHT

THE WOMAN PAYS

Her narrative ended. She had not tried to excuse herself, and she had not wept. The fire seemed like a demon, laughing at her fate.

Angel stood up and began walking around the room. His face was pale and haggard. [1] 'Why didn't you tell me this before?' he asked. 'Ah! Now I remember. You tried, but I interrupted you.'

'In the name of our love, forgive me!' she whispered with a dry mouth. 'I have forgiven you for the same. Forgive me as you are forgiven. [2] I forgive you, Angel.'

'Yes, you do.'

'But you do not forgive me?'

'O Tess, forgiveness does not apply to this case! You were one person, and now you are another.'

---

1. **haggard** : looking old and tired.
2. **Forgive me... forgiven** : this echoes a line from the Lord's Prayer.

He began to laugh. It was as unnatural and horrible as a laugh in hell.

'O stop!' cried Tess. 'Forgive me! I thought that you loved me – me, my very self! I love you, and my love will never change. How can you stop loving me?'

'The woman I have been loving is not you.'

Tess burst into a flood of self-pitying tears. He waited patiently and apathetically [1] until she stopped crying.

'I cannot stay here. I will go for a walk.' Saying this, Angel left the room.

Tess followed him, a few steps behind, with dumb [2] and vacant fidelity. [3] After a while she spoke. 'Angel, I am not the deceitful [4] woman you think I am!'

'Not deceitful, my wife, but not the same.'

'I was a child when it happened!'

'I know.'

'Then you forgive me?'

'I do forgive you, but forgiveness is not all.'

'And love me?'

He did not answer.

'Mother says it happens often, and husbands forgive wives.'

'Don't argue, Tess. Different societies have different manners. You sound like an ignorant peasant woman who does not understand social things.'

'I am only a peasant by position, not by nature!'

'That parson should have kept silent about your family. I am

---

1. **apathetically** : without interest or energy.
2. **dumb** : (here) without speaking or thinking, helpless.
3. **fidelity** : faithfulness.
4. **deceitful** : dishonest.

sure that your lack of prudence [1] is linked to your descent. [2] I thought you were a fresh child of Nature, but really you are the last descendant of a decadent [3] aristocracy!'

They walked for hours in silence. At one point, Tess said, 'You can divorce me.'

'No I can't. Tess, you know nothing of the law.'

'I don't want to cause you misery for the rest of your life. The river is down there. I will drown myself. I am not afraid.'

'I don't want to add murder to my other errors,' he replied. 'Just go back to the house and go to bed.'

She obeyed. When she lay down on her bed, Tess soon fell asleep. Later Clare returned to the house. He listened at her bedroom door and heard the rhythmic breathing of sleep. 'Thank God!' he thought. But he felt bitter too: having moved the burden of her life onto his shoulders, she was now sleeping soundly. This was partly but not completely true.

He turned away to descend the stairs and went to sleep on the sofa in the sitting room.

For the next three days, they lived together in the house. Yet they were farther apart than they had ever been. Tess made sure the meals were ready on time and tried to keep calm. Clare spent most of the day at the mill. 'Perhaps,' thought Tess, 'being together in this house day and night will finally overcome his antipathy.' [4] But Clare did not touch her. He turned away when she offered her lips for a kiss. His love for her had always been rather ideal and ethereal, [5] nothing like the strong honest

1. **prudence** : wisdom, good judgement.
2. **descent** : (here) family history.
3. **decadent** : immoral, wicked.
4. **antipathy** : dislike.
5. **ethereal** : too spiritual.

passion she had for him. Finally, Tess said to him, 'I suppose you will not live with me long, will you, Angel?' Her mouth trembled as she spoke, but she tried to control the trembling.

'We have to stay together for a few days to avoid a scandal,' Clare replied. 'But I cannot live with you long without despising [1] myself and perhaps despising you. How can we live together while that man is still alive? He is your husband in Nature. If we have children, one day they will learn about your past. Sooner or later, someone will tell them. Then they will be disgraced [2] too.'

'I never thought of that,' said Tess. 'You must go away from me, Angel. I will go home to my parents.'

'Do you want to go home?'

'I want to leave you and go home.'

'All right. We will leave here tomorrow morning and go our separate ways.'

That night at midnight, Tess heard a noise on the stairs. She saw the door of her bedroom open. Angel came in and crossed the stream of moonlight from the window. At first Tess felt a flush [3] of joy. She thought he had relented [4] after all. But then she noticed that his eyes were fixed in an unnatural stare. [5] When he reached the middle of the room, he stopped and murmured, [6] in tones of indescribable sadness, 'Dead! Dead! Dead!'

Her love for him was so deep that she could never be afraid of him. He came closer and bent over her. 'Dead! Dead! Dead!' he cried.

1. **despising** : feeling great hatred for.
2. **disgraced** : not respected.
3. **flush** : sudden rush of emotions.
4. **relented** : finally agreed.
5. **stare** : looking at Tess for a long time.
6. **murmured** : said very quietly.

He put the sheet around her and lifted her from the bed. Then he carried her across the room, murmuring, 'My poor Tess – so sweet, so good, so true!'

These words of affection brought tears to Tess's eyes. He had been so cold to her in the past three days, and her heart was hungry for love. Angel began to descend the stairs, whispering, 'My wife – dead, dead!'

He stopped and leaned over the banister. [1] 'Maybe he will drop me!' thought Tess. 'Or perhaps he will jump with me in his arms! Then we will die together.' Tess was not afraid.

He kissed her. Then, holding her more tightly, he descended the stairs and walked out into the moonlight. 'Where is he going?' Tess wondered, but still she was not afraid. 'Tomorrow we will part, perhaps for ever'. She found comfort in the fact that he now claimed her as his wife. She was his absolute possession. He could hurt her if he chose.

Ah! Now she knew what he was dreaming of! That Sunday morning when he had carried all four milkmaids over the water.

He walked to the edge of the river. 'Is he going to drown me?' thought Tess. 'Drowning will be better than parting tomorrow.' A plank [2] of wood was placed across the river as a crude bridge. Clare walked over it with Tess in his arms. The waters ran rapidly beneath them. On the other side of the river was a ruined church. Clare carried Tess into it. The empty stone coffin of an abbot [3] stood against the north wall. Clare crossed the church and gently laid Tess in the abbot's coffin. He kissed her again and sighed

1. **banister** : handrail.
2. **plank** : long flat piece.
3. **abbot** : head of an abbey.

with relief. Then he lay down on the ground beside the coffin and went to sleep.

Tess sat up in the coffin. It was too cold to leave him where he was. 'Let's walk on, darling,' she whispered, taking him by the arm. He stood up again and followed her. She took him back to the house. In the sitting room she built a fire to warm him. Then she told him to lie down on the sofa. He obeyed, and she covered him with blankets.

The next morning it was clear that Angel remembered nothing of the night before. She thought of telling him what had happened, but then decided not to. After breakfast the carriage arrived to take them as far as Nuttlebury together. Tess saw that carriage as the beginning of the end – at least a temporary end. His tenderness during the night had given her some hope for the future.

Back home in Marlott, Tess put her head on her mother's shoulder and cried, 'You told me not to tell him, but I did, and he went away!'

'O you little fool!' said Joan.

Tears ran down Tess's cheeks. The tension of the past four days had been released at last. 'I know!' she cried. 'But I could not deceive him! He was so good, and I loved him so.'

'Well, you deceived him enough to marry him first!'

'Yes. I thought that, if he could not forgive me, he could divorce me. But he told me that I don't understand the law at all. O mother, I wanted him so much, but I also wanted to be fair to him!'

'Well, well!' said Joan, with a tear in her eye. 'I don't know why my children are more stupid than other people's. Your poor

father has been telling everyone at The Pure Drop that you're married and now we will be rich.'

Meanwhile, Angel went to his family at Emminster. He told his parents nothing of his trouble. He said that he had decided to go to Brazil to start a farm there. 'Tess will stay with her family,' he said, 'and come to Brazil later, when I have a home ready for her.'

He said goodbye to his parents, then returned to the farmhouse at Wellbridge to pay the rent. He spent the night in the room where Tess had slept. In the morning, he prepared to leave for Brazil. 'O Tess!' he whispered to the empty room. 'Why didn't you tell me sooner?'

Just then he heard a knock on the door. It was Izz Huet.

'I came to see you and Mrs Clare,' she said.

'I am here alone,' said Clare. 'I am just leaving. Can I give you a ride anywhere?'

Izz blushed. 'Yes, please,' she said. 'You can take me back to the village. I don't work at Talbothay's anymore. It was so sad there after you left.'

As they drove along, Clare said, 'I am going to Brazil.'

'Does Mrs Clare like the idea?'

'I am going alone. She will join me in a year or two.'

They rode along in silence for a while.

'You look sad, Izz. Why is that?'

'I've been sad for a long time now, sir.'

'And why is that?'

Izz looked at him quickly with pain in her eyes.

'Izz! How weak of you!' he said.

They approached the village, and Clare stopped the gig. 'I am going to Brazil alone,' he said. 'I have separated from my wife for personal reasons. Perhaps I will never live with her again. I may not be able to love you, Izz, but will you go to Brazil with me?'

'Yes!'

'Do you love me very much, Izz?'

'I do!'

'More than Tess?'

She shook her head. 'No,' she murmured. 'No one could love you more than Tess did!'

Clare was silent. His heart ached. 'Forget our idle [1] talk, Izz,' he said.

Izz burst into tears.

'Be always as good and sincere as you have been today.' He helped her down from the gig.

'Heaven bless you, sir!' she cried.

That night Clare took the ship for Brazil.

It was the October after Clare and Tess had parted. Tess had left Marlott again and had found work as a milkmaid in another village. She preferred this to living on the money that Clare had left her. But then the milking stopped, and she had to look for other work. Weeks passed when she had no work and was forced to spend the money he had left her. Soon it was all gone. Angel's bank sent her another thirty pounds, but Tess sent the money to her family. Her mother had written, saying that they could not pay their debts.

Now Tess had no money. Angel had told her to go to his father if she needed money, but Tess was reluctant [2] to go. And so she moved from farm to farm, taking whatever work she could find.

1. **idle** : (here) unimportant.
2. **reluctant** : did not want.

One day Tess received a letter from Marian. Izz had told her of Tess's trouble, and Marian wrote to tell Tess that the farm where she was working now needed more help. Tess decided to join Marian. As she was walking along a country lane on her way to the new farm, a man came up behind her.

'Hello!' he said. It was the man Angel had hit outside the inn that night in December. 'Aren't you the young woman who was Mr d'Urberville's friend a few years ago?'

Tess did not reply.

'I think you should apologise for that night when your gentleman-friend hit me. What I said was true.'

Tess ran away from him. She ran into the wood and kept running until she felt safe. There, exhausted, she lay down on a pile of dry leaves and fell asleep. She woke before dawn and lay there, half-asleep. She imagined strange noises around her. She thought of her husband in a hot climate on the other side of the world, while she was here in the cold. 'All is vanity,' [1] she said to herself. But then she thought, 'No. It is worse than that: all is injustice, punishment, and death.'

That day the weather was bad, but Tess continued on her journey. The following evening, she reached the farm where Marian worked. The place was called Flintcomb-Ash, and the countryside there was dry and ugly. There were no trees, and the wind blew harshly. [2] The labour needed on this farm was the hardest kind of field work. As she approached the farm, Tess met Marian on the road. Marian was even fatter and more red-faced than before, and her clothes were old and dirty.

---

1. **vanity** : worthlessness.
2. **harshly** : with great force.

'Tess!' cried Marian. 'How cold and tired you look! But you are a gentleman's wife. It is not fair that you should live like this.'

'Please tell nobody that I am married. I want to work. Do they still need help here?'

'Yes, but it's a miserable place. The work is hard and the weather is bad.'

'You work here, Marian.'

'Yes. I started drinking after you left Talbothay's. It's my only comfort, but, because of my drinking, I can only get the roughest [1] work now.'

The farmer was away, so Marian introduced Tess to the farmer's wife, who was glad to give her a job. Then Tess went into town and found lodgings. [2] That night, in her room, she wrote a letter to her mother, but she did not tell her about the poor conditions in which she was now living. She did not wish to give anyone reason to criticise her husband.

The work at Flintcomb-Ash was very hard indeed. They had to harvest swedes. [3] The cattle had eaten all the leaves above ground, so the field was brown and desolate. The workers had to dig the swedes out of the stony earth. Day after day they worked in the wind and the rain. Then the snow came, and the air was freezing cold.

One day, the farmer returned and came to watch the women working in the field. He stood beside Tess, watching her with interest. When she looked up, she saw that he was the man Angel had hit, the man she had run away from on the road. 'You thought

---

1. **roughest** : most difficult.
2. **lodgings** : rented rooms.
3. **swedes** : hard root-vegetables that grow underground.

you had escaped me when you ran away that day, but now you are working on my farm! I think you should apologise to me,' he said.

'And I think you should apologise to me,' replied Tess.

From then on, life on the farm was even more difficult for Tess than it had been before.

One evening, Marian and Tess sat together, talking about the old life at Talbothay's. Marian was drinking gin, and, as always when she drank, her thoughts turned to love.

'I did love him so!' said Marian. 'I didn't mind when he married you, but this news about Izz is too bad!'

'What news?'

'O dear! Izz told me not to tell you, but I can't help it. [1] He asked Izz to go to Brazil with him.'

Tess went pale. 'And she refused?'

'I don't know. Anyway, he changed his mind.'

That night, Tess tried to write a letter to Angel, but she could not. How could she write to him when he had asked Izz to go to Brazil with him so soon after their parting? Why had he not written to her? She thought perhaps she ought to go to his parents in Emminster. She could go to his parents' house, ask them for news of him, and express her grief [2] at his silence.

The following Sunday, she dressed in her best clothes and set out for Emminster very early in the morning. As she walked through the crisp [3] morning air, her heart was full of hope. 'I will tell his mother my whole history. Perhaps that lady will pity me

---

1. **I can't help it** : I can't prevent myself.

2. **grief** : (here) great sadness.
3. **crisp** : (here) cold.

and help me to win Angel back.' Gradually the landscape became gentler and greener, the fields smaller. At noon she stood on the hill above Emminster.

All the hope she had felt on the journey now drained [1] away. She walked timidly to the door of Reverend Clare's house and rang the bell. No one answered. Then she realised they must all be at church. 'I will walk up the hill and wait until they have finished their lunch,' thought Tess. As she was walking up the hill, the church doors opened and the congregation emerged.

A young man, walking behind Tess, began speaking to his companion. Tess noticed that his voice was very like Angel's. 'Look!' said he. 'That's Mercy Chant walking up the hill. Let's join her.'

Tess had heard that name before. Angel's parents had wanted him to marry Mercy Chant. Tess looked up the hill and saw a young woman in plain dark clothes.

'Every time I see Mercy,' continued the young man behind her, 'I think what a great mistake Angel made when he married that milkmaid.'

'It certainly was a mistake,' said his companion. 'But Angel always had strange ideas.'

Tess hurried back along the road to Flintcomb-Ash. She no longer had the courage to speak to Mr and Mrs Clare. The brothers were so cold and unpleasant. And they clearly did not love poor Angel. She grieved [2] for the beloved man whose conventional ideas had caused all her recent sorrow.

---

1. **drained** : (here) went.
2. **grieved** : felt great sadness.

Go back to the text

1 **Answer the following questions.**

1. Angel said, 'the woman I have been loving is not you.' What did he mean by this?
2. While they were walking what solution did Tess have to their problem?
3. In what way did Tess and Angel's love for each other differ?
4. What made Tess suggest that she should go home to her parents?
5. What is the symbolic effect of placing Tess in the coffin?
6. Why did Tess still have some hope for the future?
7. What reason did Angel give for going to Brazil?
8. Why did Tess have no money?
9. How did Tess find the job at Flintcomb-Ash?
10. Why did meeting the owner of farm make life more difficult for Tess?

2 **In the box below there are some of the characters from the novel. In Part A, write the name of the character to complete each sentence. You do not need to use all the characters' names. In Part B, indicate which character is the subject of each sentence.**

> Angel   Alec   Marian   Tess   Reverend Clare
> Mrs d'Urberville   Jack   Joan

A

1. Marian was a friend of ....
2. .... was the father-in-law of Tess.
3. .... was the mother of Tess.
4. .... was the husband of Tess.
5. Joan was the wife of ....
6. Alec was the son of ....
7. .... celebrated with a drink when he found out the truth about his family.

B

1. Her husband had lived in London.   ....
2. He carried his wife across a river.   ....
3. He had two brothers.   ....
4. She told her friend about a job.   ....
5. She thought her daughter was foolish.   ....
6. He was not at home when his daughter-in-law called. ....
7. His mother was an invalid.   ....
8. He embarrassed his daughter.   ....
9. He was responsible for Tess's situation.   ....

Grammar

Past Perfect – Revision

Use **had** plus **past participle**.

The **Past Simple** is used to talk about single past events.
*Tom **arrived** at the station.*
*Catherine **was** nervous.*

The **Past Perfect** is used to describe an event **before** a point in time in the past. Only use the **Past Perfect**, if it is necessary to establish the order of actions.
*When Tom **arrived** at the station the train **had** already **left**.*
*Catherine **was** nervous because she **had** never **flown** before.*

3 Match a phrase from A with a phrase from B. Then make complete sentences using the Past Perfect. In each case use *because* to join the two sentences. The first has been completed as an example.

A

1. Angel's face looks pale and haggard.
2. Angel leaves the room.
3. Angel turns away.
4. Tess's heart is hungry for love.

5. Tess can't deceive him.
6. Tess finds work in another village.
7. Tess sends money to her family.
8. No one answers the door.

B

A   Tess bursts into tears.
B   Tess leaves Marlott again.
C   They go to church.
D   Tess tells him the truth about her past.
E   Tess's mother writes a letter saying that they could not pay their debts.
F   Tess offers him her lips.
G   Angel has been cold to her for some days.
H   Angel is so good to her.

0.   *Angel's face looked pale and haggard because Tess had told him the truth about her past.*

1.   ....

2.   ....

3.   ....

4.   ....

5.   ....

6.   ....

7.   ....

4 In this chapter Angel is described as being a man of 'conventional ideas.' What does this mean? Do you agree with this opinion? Use extracts from Chapter Eight to support your views.

5 In Chapter Eight, Tess writes to her mother from her lodgings. Write Tess's letter in 120-180 words. Use examples of the Past Perfect where possible. In the letter talk about the following events:

* Moving away from Marlott
* Moving from farm to farm in search of work
* Receiving a letter from Marian
* Meeting a familiar man on a country lane
* Arriving at Flintcomb-Ash
* The work on the farm

Before you go on

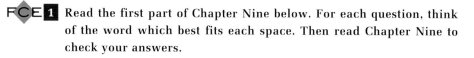

1 Read the first part of Chapter Nine below. For each question, think of the word which best fits each space. Then read Chapter Nine to check your answers.

As Tess walked (**1**)............... from Emminster to Flintcomb-Ash, she saw a (**2**)............... of people around a barn. 'What is happening?' she (**3**)............... a woman there.
'We've all come to listen to the preaching,' the woman (**4**)............... .
'They say his sermons are very fiery!'
Tess went closer to the barn. She could not see the speaker, (**5**)............... she could (**6**)............... him. He (**7**)............... calling sinners to repentance, warning them about the fires of hell. Then he began to tell his (**8**)............... history. He said he had been the (**9**)............... of sinners. Then one day he (**10**)............... a clergyman – the Reverend Clare of Emminster – who tried to call him to repentance. At first he (**11**)............... ignored Mr Clare's preaching, but finally he was converted and gave (**12**)............... his evil ways. The voice was (**13**)............... startling to Tess than its message. It was the voice of Alec d'Urberville. She moved (**14**)............... the crowd to the door of the barn, her heart (**15**)............... in suspense. Then she saw him, standing before the crowd in a flood of afternoon sunlight.

CHAPTER NINE

THE CONVERT

As Tess walked back from Emminster to Flintcomb-Ash, she saw a crowd of people around a barn. 'What is happening?' she asked a woman there.

'We've all come to listen to the preaching,' the woman replied. 'They say his sermons [1] are very fiery!' [2]

Tess went closer to the barn. She could not see the speaker, but she could hear him. He was calling sinners to repentance, [3] warning them about the fires of hell. Then he began to tell his own history. He said he had been the greatest of sinners. Then one day he met a clergyman – the Reverend Clare of Emminster – who tried to call him to repentance. At first he had ignored Mr Clare's preaching, but finally he was converted [4] and gave up his evil ways.

---

1. **sermons** : the speeches given by a priest or other religious person.

2. **fiery** : passionate.

3. **repentance** : regret for wrong doing.

4. **converted** : persuaded to repent.

126

The voice was more startling to Tess than its message. It was the voice of Alec d'Urberville. She moved through the crowd to the door of the barn, her heart beating in suspense. Then she saw him, standing before the crowd in the afternoon sunlight.

Till this moment, she had never seen or heard from d'Urberville since her departure from Trantridge. His appearance had changed. The moustache was gone, and his clothes were more sober. For a moment Tess doubted that it was really him. Then there could be no doubt that her seducer stood before her.

There was something grotesque about solemn words of scripture coming out of that mouth. Less than four years earlier she had heard that voice use the same powers of persuasion for a very different purpose. Everything about him was transformed, and yet the difference was not great. The aggressive [1] energy of his animal passions was now used for an equally aggressive religious fanaticism.

'But perhaps I am being unfair,' thought Tess. 'Wicked men do sometimes turn away from wickedness to save their souls.'

Just then, Alec recognised her. The fire suddenly went out of him. His lips trembled. His eyes avoided hers. Tess hurried away from the barn.

As she walked away from the barn, her back seemed sensitive to eyes watching her, his eyes. She walked quickly, desperate to get as far away from him as possible. 'Bygones will never be bygones,' she thought bitterly, 'until I am a bygone myself. [2]

Then she heard his footsteps behind her. 'Leave me alone!' she cried.

1. **aggressive** : offensive.
2. **Bygones ... myself** : 'Let bygones be bygones' is an idiom meaning 'forget what is past (gone by)'. Here Tess thinks she will never be free of the past until she is dead.

'I deserve that. But, Tess, of all the people in the world, you – the woman I wronged so much – are the one I should try to save!'

'Have you saved yourself?' asked Tess with bitter irony.

'Heaven has saved me, and it can save you too!'

'How dare you talk to me like this, when you know what harm you've done me! I don't believe in your conversion or your religion!'

'Why not?'

Tess looked into his eyes and said slowly, 'Because a better man than you does not believe in it.'

'Don't look at me like that!' said Alec abruptly. [1] His animal passions were subdued, [2] but they were not dead.

'I beg your pardon,' [3] said Tess, and she suddenly felt, as she had felt often before, that she was doing something wrong simply by inhabiting the body that Nature had given her.

He told her to cover her face with her veil. She did so, and they walked together as far as the intersection of the roads. On the way, she told him about the first of her troubles. He was shocked to hear what she had suffered. 'I knew nothing about it till now!' he said at last. Then they reached the intersection called Cross-in-Hand, where there was a stone pillar with the image of a human hand on it.

'You will see me again,' he said.

'No,' she answered. 'Don't come near me again!'

'I will think. But before we part, come here. Place your hand upon this pillar and swear that you will never tempt me.'

'How can you ask such a thing?'

'Do it.'

Tess, half-frightened, put her hand on the stone and swore.

---

1. **abruptly** : suddenly and unexpectedly.

2. **subdued** : controlled.

3. **beg your pardon** : excuse me.

They parted ways, and Tess went on alone towards Flintcomb-Ash. After a few minutes, she passed a solitary shepherd. 'What is the meaning of that stone pillar at Cross-in-Hand?' she asked. 'Was it ever a Holy Cross?'

'No! It is a thing of bad omen, [1] Miss. It was put there in old times by the family of a criminal who was tortured there. They nailed his hand to a post and then they hanged him. His bones are buried beneath the pillar. They say he sold his soul to the devil, and that his ghost walks at night.'

A cold February wind blew across the dull [2] brown field. Tess worked monotonously. She did not notice the figure approaching her. D'Urberville came up to her and said, 'I want to speak to you, Tess.'

'I told you not to come near me!' cried Tess.

'When we last met, I was concerned for the condition of your soul. I didn't ask you about your worldly condition. I see now that your life is difficult. Perhaps this is in part my fault.'

She did not reply but continued working as before.

'I want to recompense you for the suffering I have caused. My mother died recently, and The Slopes is now mine. I intend to sell the house and go to Africa as a missionary. Will you be my wife and go with me?'

'No!'

'Why not?' He sounded disappointed. He felt it was his duty to marry her, but it was also his desire.

'I have no affection for you. I love somebody else,' said Tess.

'Have you no sense of what is morally right?'

---

1. **omen** : sign.
2. **dull** : without colour.

'Don't say that! Besides, I cannot marry you because I am married to him.'

'Ah!' he exclaimed. 'Who is your husband?'

'I won't tell you,' said Tess. 'No one here knows that I am married.'

'And where is he? Why is he not with you?'

'Because I told him about you.'

'He abandoned you?'

'Go away! For me and for my husband, go in the name of your own Christianity!'

Just then the farmer rode into the field. 'Get back to work!' he shouted angrily at Tess.

'Don't speak to her like that!' cried Alec.

'Go – I beg you!' said Tess.

'I can't leave you with that tyrant.'

'He won't hurt me. He's not in love with me.'

'All right,' said Alec reluctantly. 'Goodbye.'

When he was gone, Tess imagined herself married to Alec and all his wealth. 'But no,' she thought. 'I could never marry him: I dislike him so much.'

That night she wrote a letter to Clare. But then she remembered that he had asked Izz to go to Brazil. Perhaps he did not care for her at all. Instead of sending the letter, she put it in her box.

One day, when Tess was alone in her lodgings, Alec appeared at the door. He came in, sat down, and said, 'It's no use. I cannot resist my attraction to you. Ever since I saw you that Sunday, I have been thinking about you all the time. I was an enthusiastic convert, but now I have returned to my old way of thinking. Sometimes I think you are like Eve in Milton's

Paradise Lost, [1] and I am the serpent. You should pray for me, Tess.'

'I cannot pray for you. I don't believe that God will alter [2] his plans for me.'

Alec asked her about her beliefs, and she repeated things that Angel had said to her. They were arguments against the kind of religion preached by Angel's father, the same that Alec now preached. She remembered every word, although she did not understand it all. Alec listened thoughtfully to the arguments.

'Today I should be preaching at Casterbridge Fair, but instead I am here. Give me one kiss, Tess. Then I will go away.'

'No! I am a married woman! Leave me!'

'All right,' he said, and he did feel ashamed. Nevertheless, his religious sense of guilt had been weakened by the arguments that Tess had repeated to him. As he left the cottage, he said to himself, 'That clever fellow never thought that, by telling her those things, he might be helping me to get her back!'

Time passed and Alec's passion for Tess grew. He came to see her often. 'Be mine, Tess,' he often said to her. 'I'll give you all the money you want. I'll give you a life of ease.' But Tess refused.

In March, the farmer hired a threshing machine. [3] He always gave Tess the hardest jobs. Now she had to stand on the back of the machine from dawn to dusk, in clouds of dust and noise, untying the sheaves and feeding corn into the machine. It was back-breaking [4] work. Often she looked up and saw Alec, elegantly

---

1. **Paradise Lost** : an epic poem based on the story of Adam and Eve in Genesis, written by the English poet John Milton (1608-74) and published in 1667.
2. **alter** : change.
3. **threshing machine** : a machine which removes the seeds from the corn.
4. **back-breaking** : exhausting.

dressed, waiting for her by the hedge. He had stopped preaching now and stopped wearing the sober clothes of a religious man.

In desperation, Tess wrote to Angel:

'MY OWN HUSBAND – Let me call you so – even though I am an unworthy wife. I must cry to you in my trouble. I have no one else! I am so exposed to temptation, Angel. Please come home to me now, before something terrible happens. You are right to be angry with me. But please come to me, even if I do not deserve it. Angel, I live entirely for you. I love you. I don't blame you for going away. But I am so desolate without you, my darling. Save me from what threatens me!

Your faithful heartbroken
TESS

Angel Clare looked out over the wide plain. He was sitting on the mule that had carried him from the interior of South America to the coast. His experiences of this strange land had been sad. He had been very ill shortly after arriving here and had never fully recovered. Now he had given up hope of starting a farm here. Many other farmers from England had suffered and died in Brazil. In twelve months, Angel's mind had aged twelve years. He now valued the pathos[1] of life more than its beauty. Now he saw that the true beauty or ugliness of a person lay in his intentions: his true history was not the things he had done but rather the things he had willed.[2]

Viewing Tess in this light, he regretted his judgement of her. His travelling companion on this last journey had been an Englishman who had lived in many different countries. They had talked together frequently and intimately. Eventually, Angel had told him

1. **pathos** : pity, sadness.
2. **willed** : tried to make something happen by using someone's mental power.

about the sorrows of his marriage. To the other's cosmopolitan [1] mind, Tess's deviation [2] from the social norm was insignificant. He had said, 'What Tess had been is much less important than what she will become. I think you were wrong to leave her.'

Soon afterwards, the Englishman caught a fever and died. Clare began to feel remorse [3] about his treatment of Tess. Izz's words were repeated over and over again in his mind: *No one could love you more than Tess did!'*

As he thought about these things, Tess's letter was travelling over the ocean towards him. She had sent it to his parents: that was the only address she had. They had forwarded [4] it to him. But in the meantime, Tess was feeling sad and discouraged. She often thought, 'He will never return!' Then one day in April her sister Liza-Lu came to Flintcomb-Ash. Liza-Lu had grown so tall and thin that Tess hardly recognised her at first.

'Is something wrong at home?' asked Tess.

'O Tess! Our parents are ill and we don't know what to do!' The poor girl began to cry.

Tess and Liza-Lu returned to Marlott that night. Soon after Jack Durbeyfield died. Her mother and the other children were all in deep distress because of her father's death. The next day, the owner of their cottage told them to leave by the end of the week. Now that Jack was dead, they had no right to stay there. Joan said they should go to Kingsbere, where the d'Urbervilles were buried. Tess agreed, though she knew that it was a foolish plan.

On their last evening in Marlott, Tess sat by the window, watching the rain outside. All their possessions were packed. Tess's mother and the children had gone to bed. Suddenly there

---

1. **cosmopolitan** : having wide experience of the world.
2. **deviation** : not following.
3. **remorse** : regret.
4. **forwarded** : sent.

was a knock on the door. When Tess opened it, she saw Alec standing outside in a white raincoat. 'Ah,' she said. 'I thought I heard a carriage.'

'I came on horseback,' said Alec. 'Perhaps you heard the d'Urberville coach. Do you know that legend?'

'No. Someone was going to tell me once, but he didn't.'

'It is rather depressing,' said Alec, coming in. 'If a d'Urberville hears the coach it is a bad omen. One of the family abducted [1] a beautiful woman. She tried to escape from the coach in which he abducted her. In the struggle, he killed her, or she killed him – I forget which. I see you are all packed and ready to go.'

'Yes. Tomorrow we go to Kingsbere.'

'Listen, Tess,' said d'Urberville. 'Bring your family to The Slopes. The cottage that was once the chicken farm is empty now. I will have it cleaned and painted, and you can live there. I want to help you.'

'No,' said Tess.

'Damn it, Tess, don't be a fool. I shall expect you at The Slopes tomorrow.'

When he had gone, Tess took a pen and wrote the following letter: 'O why have you treated me so badly, Angel? I do not deserve it. I can never forgive you! You know that I did not intend to wrong you. You are cruel! I will try to forget you. T.'

'Who was your visitor last night, Tess?' asked her mother the next morning. 'Was it your husband?'

'No. My husband will never come.'

She had said that it was not her husband. Yet Tess was becoming more and more aware that in a physical sense this man alone was her husband.

---

1. **abducted** : kidnapped.

When Tess and her family arrived at Kingsbere, they found the lodgings they had booked were already taken. Tess and Liza-Lu ran through the streets, looking for other rooms, but none was free. They returned to the cart, where their mother and the children were waiting with all their boxes and furniture.

'Never mind!' said Joan. 'Unload everything here!' The cart was standing outside Kingsbere Church. 'I suppose your own family tombs are your own property? Then we will sleep in the churchyard!'

They carried the old four-poster bed into the churchyard and put it by the south wall of the church. Above it was a stained-glass [1] window, in which they could see the d'Urberville emblems [2] – the lion and castle familiar to them from their own seal and spoon. Joan drew the curtains around the bed and put the children inside. Then she and Liza-Lu went to find some food.

Tess went into the church. A figure lay upon one of the d'Urberville tombs. Suddenly Tess realised that this figure was not marble but a living man. It moved. The shock was so great that she nearly fainted. Alec jumped off the tomb and supported her. 'Tess, I – a sham [3] d'Urberville – can do more for you than all these real ones. Now command me. What shall I do?'

'Go away!' she cried.

'All right. I'll go and find your mother. But you will be civil to me yet!'

When he had gone, she bent down on the entrance to the vaults below and whispered, 'Why am I on the wrong side of this door?'

1. **stained-glass** : glass of different colours making a picture in the church window.
2. **emblems** : symbolic images, in this case the castle argent and the lion rampant that are symbols of the d'Urberville family.
3. **sham** : not genuine.

Go back to the text

1 For the following questions, put the words into the correct order and then answer them.

1. to/Alec/who/repent/convinced

.... ?

2. Alec/did/how/react/he/when/Tess/saw

.... ?

3. Tess/believe/why/that/did/not/Alec/had/repented

.... ?

4. the meaning/was/of/what/the stone pillar

.... ?

5. did/Alec/do/want/Africa/to/what/in

.... ?

6. made/Tess/to/Angel/what/write

.... ?

7. was/happy/new/Angel/his/why/not/life/with

.... ?

8. family/the cottage/did/Tess's/why/leave

.... ?

9. is/the legend/what/of/coach/the d'Urberville

.... ?

10. did/Tess/her/family/who/and/on/find/lying/the tomb

.... ?

2 In the box are some characters from Chapter Nine. For each question decide which character is being referred to. Write the character's initial next to each of the actions.

T	Tess	**AN**	Angel
J	Joan	**LL**	Liza-Lu
R	Reverend Clare	**JK**	Jack
AL	Alec		

☐ **1.** He was shocked to see her.

☐ **2.** She hadn't seen Alec for nearly four years.

☐ **3.** Despite his new morality his aggression and passion were apparent.

☐ **4.** He was not very happy with his new life.

☐ **5.** She doubted that Alec had really converted.

☐ **6.** He died soon after Tess returned home.

☐ **7.** She suggested that they should go to Kingsbere.

☐ **8.** He lay upon a tomb in Kingsbere Church.

☐ **9.** She had become very tall and thin.

☐ **10.** She suggested that they sleep in the churchyard.

3 **The text below is a summary of Thomas Hardy's last novel, _Jude the Obscure_. It is another story of love and complex relationships. Seven phrases have been removed from the text. Choose from phrases A-H the one which fits each gap. There is an example at the beginning (0).**

In this novel Hardy dramatises the conflict between spiritual and physical needs. The story follows Jude Fawley's life from (**0**).....<u>C</u>..... to his miserable, early death. His passionate nature entangles him in a marriage to Anabella, an insensitive woman (**1**)............., then he deserts them both. Jude then falls in love with his cousin, Sue Bridehead, an intelligent, sensitive but nervous person. However, Sue (**2**)........... schoolteacher called Phillotson instead. The marriage is not a happy one. She finds her husband physically unattractive, (**3**)............ . Jude and Sue both obtain divorces. Unfortunately Sue feels guilty about leaving her husband and cannot bring herself to marry Jude. Consequently they (**4**)............ . Scorned and rejected by society, they have three children. At home things go terribly wrong. The three children (**5**)............, a grotesque boy, also called Jude, who then hangs himself. Sue goes back to her husband and Jude returns to his wife (**6**)............ . Both _Tess of the d'Urbervilles_ and _Jude the Obscure_ are tragedies about a successful society that, in this case, scorns outsiders like women and ambitious working men.

A because their relationship is ruined by this tragedy

B are killed by Anabella's son

C his boyhood dreams of intellectual achievement

D decide to live together

E who gives birth to a son

F marries an old and decaying

G so she returns to Jude

H as he must return to London

4 **Tess is the victim of the story, but is there a hero? Who do you think the hero of the story is? And who is the villain? Find evidence from the text to support your ideas.**

Before you go on

T: GRADE 8

1 Topic – Living standards

In *Tess of the d'Urbervilles* written more than 100 years ago, Tess and her family have very difficult lives. However, in Chapter Ten she lives like a lady for a short period. Choose a picture which shows what the place where you live was like in the past, and a photo of what it looks like now. Find how the place you live in has changed. Use the following questions to help you.

A Has the place changed a lot? How has it changed?

B What kind of jobs did people do in the past? How did they live?

C What kind of jobs do people do now? How do they live?

2 Read the text below. Use the word given in capitals at the end of each line to form a word that fits in the space in the same line. There is an example at the beginning **(0)**. Now listen to the first part of Chapter Ten to check your answers.

In May Angel Clare returned to England with two letters in his pocket. He went **(0)**......*briefly*...... to his parents at Emminster and then hired a gig and set out to find his wife. His parents were shocked to see how much he had changed. His face was thin, and his eyes were **(1)**....................... . He wore a beard now, which made him look much **(2)**....................... than he was. Clare passed the stone pillar at Cross-in-Hand and went on to Flintcomb-Ash, to the address from which her letters had been sent. None of the villagers there could remember anyone called Mrs Clare: they had known Tess only by her **(3)**.................... name. Clare found this **(4)**.................... .
Her refusal to use his name, like her refusal to go to his father for help, showed a **(5)**.................... sense of their total **(6)**.................... . And here for the first time Clare understood the hardships she had suffered in his **(7)**....................... . The farm-workers told him that Tess had gone to her parents in Marlott, and so he continued his journey.
Clare's gig entered the **(8)**..................... valley in which his dear Tess had been **(9)**..................... and descended the green slopes to the village of Marlott.
The villagers told him that Mr Durbeyfield was **(10)**...................., and Mrs Durbeyfield and the children had left Marlott.

BRIEF
ANXIETY
OLD
CHRIST
COURAGE
DIGNITY
SEPARATE
ABSENT
LOVE
BIRTH
DIE

CHAPTER TEN

FULFILMENT

n May Angel Clare returned to England with two letters in his pocket. He went briefly to his parents at Emminster and then hired a gig and set out to find his wife. His parents were shocked to see how much he had changed. His face was thin, and his eyes were anxious. He wore a beard now, which made him look much older than he was.

Clare passed the stone pillar at Cross-in-Hand and went on to Flintcomb-Ash, to the address from which her letters had been sent. None of the villagers there could remember anyone called Mrs Clare: they had known Tess only by her Christian name. Clare found this discouraging. Her refusal to use his name, like her refusal to go to his father for help, showed a dignified sense of their total separation. And here for the first time Clare understood the hardships [1] she had suffered in his absence. The farm workers

---

1. **hardships** : great difficulties.

told him that Tess had gone to her parents in Marlott, and so he continued his journey.

Clare's gig entered the lovely valley in which his dear Tess had been born and descended the green slopes to the village of Marlott. The villagers told him that Mr Durbeyfield was dead, and Mrs Durbeyfield and the children had left Marlott.

Clare began to despair. He went for a walk through the village to plan his next step. [1] He passed by the field where Tess and the village women had danced all those years ago. He passed through the graveyard and saw John Durbeyfield's grave. On the gravestone were engraved these words:

John Durbeyfield, rightly d'Urberville,

direct descendant of Sir Pagan d'Urberville,

a knight of William the Conqueror.

HOW THE MIGHTY ARE FALLEN

The people who now lived in the Durbeyfield's cottage gave Clare Joan's present address. He hired a gig and went there as fast as he could.

Clare had never met Joan before. When she answered the door, he noticed that she was a good-looking woman in respectable widow's dress. She looked at him nervously. He told her he was Tess's husband, and that he was looking for Tess. Joan was reluctant to give him the address. She said she was sure that Tess did not wish him to find her. But Clare did not believe her. He remembered Tess's first letter. 'Please tell me her address, Mrs Durbeyfield, in kindness to a sad and lonely man!'

Finally Joan told him that Tess was at Sandbourne – a fashionable seaside resort near Egdon Heath. Clare thanked her and

---

1. **step** : (here) action which is part of a plan.

hurried away to catch the next train for Sandbourne.

Joan had been unable to give Clare an address. All she knew was the name of the town in which Tess was now living. Clare walked down the fashionable streets of Sandbourne, looking at the shops and restaurants, he wondered what Tess – his young wife, a farm-girl – could be doing here. There were no cows to milk, no fields to harvest. He went to the post office and asked if they knew the address of Mrs Clare. The postman shook his head.

'Or Miss Durbeyfield?' asked Angel.

'No. But there is someone named d'Urberville at The Herons.'

The postman gave Clare directions to a small elegant hotel.

Clare rang the doorbell of The Herons. The proprietor [1] – Mrs Brooks – answered the door and said, yes, there was a Mrs d'Urberville in the house. She asked Angel to wait in the sitting-room and went upstairs to call Tess.

'O dear!' thought Angel. 'What will she think of me? I have changed so much.'

Then he heard Tess's step on the stair, and his heart beat painfully.

Tess appeared at the door. She was not at all as he had expected. She wore a grey cashmere dressing gown. Her whole appearance was that of an elegant lady with plenty of money.

'Tess,' he said. 'Can you forgive me for going away?'

'It's too late,' Tess replied, her eyes shining unnaturally.

'I didn't understand, but now I do.'

'Too late! Too late!' she said, waving her hand impatiently like someone in great pain. 'Don't come close to me, Angel!'

'Don't you love me anymore? I know I look different. I've been ill. Please come with me.'

1. **proprietor** : owner.

'I waited and waited for you,' she cried in her musical voice. 'But you did not come! He kept saying, "Your husband will never come back!" He helped my family. He won me back to him. Now I hate him, because he lied. You have come back! But it's too late!''

Angel stood still and silent for a minute when he heard this. Then he said, 'Ah! It is my fault!'

She ran upstairs. After a while he left the house.

Mrs Brooks had heard part of this conversation from her room, which was opposite the sitting room. Curious, she went upstairs and looked through the keyhole of the door to the d'Urbervilles' apartment. Through the keyhole she saw the breakfast things she had brought them earlier, and she saw Tess, lying on the floor, weeping. She heard Alec's voice ask, 'What's the matter?' Tess leapt up and replied with passionate fury. Afraid of being caught listening at the door, Mrs Brooks went downstairs quickly and quietly and sat in her room. All was now quiet in the d'Urbervilles' room above. After a while, she saw Tess leave the house.

Mrs Brooks rested her head on the back of her chair. Looking up, she noticed a spot the size of a wafer [1] in the middle of the white ceiling. As she looked, the spot grew to the size of a hand. It was red. The rectangular white ceiling, with this red spot in the middle, looked like a gigantic heart.

Mrs Brooks ran upstairs and listened at the d'Urbervilles' door. The only sound was a regular beat: drip, drip, drip.

She opened the door, and there, on the bed, she saw Alec d'Urberville in a pool of blood with the bread-knife in his heart.

'Angel! Angel!' called Tess. Angel turned round and saw her

---

1. **wafer** : a thin biscuit, which symbolizes the body of Christ in the Eucharist.

running towards him. She was so pale and breathless that he took her hand and led her off the road into the forest. When they were hidden among the trees, he looked at her.

'I have killed him!' she said, and a pitiful white smile lit her face.

'What?'

'I never loved him at all as I love you! I thought you didn't love me anymore, so I went back to him. But now I have killed him, so say you love me, Angel!'

'I love you,' he said, holding her tightly in his arms. 'But have you really killed him?'

'Yes. I was crying after you left – my heart was breaking! He asked me why, and I became so furious I screamed at him. Then he ridiculed me for loving you, and he called you terrible names. [1] And then I did it!'

He kissed her and said, 'I will not desert you! I will protect you, love, whatever you have done!'

At first, Clare did not believe that she had killed d'Urberville. Perhaps she had tried to kill him. Clare's horror at her impulse was mixed with amazement at the strength of her love for himself. Her love seemed to have extinguished [2] her moral sense. Now that she was with Clare again, she seemed content. Nothing else seemed to matter. He looked at her face and thought of the d'Urberville coach. Perhaps the legend arose because the d'Urbervilles had been known to do these things.

They walked deeper into the forest. For miles and miles they walked, happy to be together alone at last. At noon they came to an inn. Angel told Tess to stay hidden among the trees. He entered the inn and returned with enough food for two days. They ate in the forest then walked on. Towards evening they came to a

---

1. **called you terrible names** : laughed at you, insulted you.
2. **extinguished** : ended the existence of something.

large house. It stood alone in the forest. On the gate was a sign saying, 'Furnished mansion for rent.'

'It is empty!' said Tess. 'We could spend the night here.'

Some of the windows were open. Tess and Angel climbed in through a ground-floor window. They went upstairs and into one of the bedrooms. It was a large room full of old-fashioned furniture. In the middle of it was a huge four-poster bed. [1] Angel put down his bag and the package of food. He sat on the bed and said, 'Rest at last!'

As they ate, Tess told him about the night he carried her across the river and put her in the abbot's coffin.

'Why didn't you tell me the next day?' he asked.

'Don't think about the past,' she said. 'Just think of the present. Who knows what tomorrow will bring?'

The next day was cold and rainy. They stayed in the mansion all day and the next night. Angel went out and bought some more food at a shop some miles away. They stayed in the mansion for five days. They spoke of the past, but only the distant past, before their wedding day. On the fifth day, Clare said, 'We should leave this place.'

'Why?' asked Tess. 'We are so happy here. Inside this house is contentment. [2] Outside is trouble.'

It was true. Inside was love, forgiveness, and peace. Outside was danger. 'I know, my love,' said Clare. 'But soon someone will come to clean the house. We must not be found here.'

The next day was sunny. They travelled north. Soon they came to the edge of the forest. They decided to sleep in the afternoon and continue their journey at night, under the cover of darkness. They

---

1. **four-poster bed** : a bed with a column at each corner which supports a canopy over the bed.
2. **contentment** : happiness.

passed through a silent sleeping town and on to the plain beyond. After walking for hours, they came upon a great stone structure.

'What is it?' asked Tess. It was made of enormous blocks of stone. Some stood erect, others were lying on the ground.

'It's Stonehenge!' said Clare.

'The pagan temple?'

'Yes. It is older than the centuries, older than the d'Urbervilles!'

Tess lay down on one of the stone slabs. [1] 'I don't want to go any further,' she said.

Clare knelt down beside her. 'Are you tired? The stone you are lying on looks like an altar.'

'Angel, if anything happens to me, will you take care of Liza-Lu?'

'I will.'

'She is so good and simple and pure. Please marry her if you lose me.'

'If I lose you, I lose everything!'

Gradually the sky grew paler and the great blocks of stone stood dark against it.

'Did they sacrifice to God here?' asked Tess.

'No. I think they worshipped the sun.' [2]

'Angel, do you believe we will meet again after death?'

He did not answer but kissed her instead.

'O! I fear that means no!' she cried with tears in her eyes.

She clasped [3] his hand, but after a while he felt her grip relax in sleep.

---

1. **slabs** : big, rectangular pieces.
2. **worshipped the sun** : believed that the sun was God.
3. **clasped** : held tightly.

The great plain was now visible in the morning light. The sun rose behind the Sun stone. Light bathed the Stone of Sacrifice. Clare saw something moving in the distance. He heard footsteps behind him. To his right and his left he saw men moving towards them. So her story was true! Clare leapt up and looked for a weapon.

'It's no use, sir,' said one of the men. 'There are sixteen of us.'

Tess woke up. 'What is it, Angel?' she asked. 'Have they come for me?'

'Yes, dearest.'

'I am almost glad,' she said. 'This happiness was too much. I have had enough.' Then she turned to the policeman and said, 'I am ready.'

On a warm July morning, Angel Clare and Liza-Lu climbed the hill above the city of Wintoncester. It was a fine old city, once the capital of Wessex County. Clare and his sister-in-law walked hand-in-hand, their heads bent with sorrow. She was taller and thinner than Tess, but she had the same eloquent eyes. When they reached the summit of the hill they looked out over the landscape and the Gothic spires of Wintoncester. The cathedral bells rang eight o'clock. Clare and Liza-Lu started at the sound. They stared down at a large ugly building in the middle of the city. On one of the building's towers stood a flagpole. A few minutes after the hour had struck, something moved slowly up the flagpole. It was a black flag.

'Justice' was done. The President of the Immortals had ended his sport [1] with Tess. The d'Urberville knights and ladies slept on in their tombs unawares. Clare and Liza-Lu knelt down on the ground as if in prayer. They remained there a long time. Then they rose, joined hands again, and went on.

---

1. **sport** : joke, fun.

Go back to the text

1 Decide if the following statements are true (T) or false (F).

	T	F
1. Angel hadn't physically changed.	☐	☐
2. Angel found out where Tess was from her mother Joan.	☐	☐
3. Angel was surprised to find Tess living in Sandbourne.	☐	☐
4. Tess's appearance was that of a simple woman.	☐	☐
5. Mrs Brooks found Alec dead on the bedroom floor.	☐	☐
6. Seeing Angel again made Tess hate Alec.	☐	☐
7. Tess had planned to kill Alec.	☐	☐
8. Tess and Angel took refuge in a pagan temple.	☐	☐
9. Tess gave herself up to the police.	☐	☐
10. Angel and Liza-Lu attended the execution.	☐	☐

Grammar

The Third Conditional

Use the third conditional to talk about something in the past which **cannot be changed** now.

*If I **had revised**, I **would have passed** the exam.*
(But I didn't revise and I failed the exam.)

If + Past Perfect, would have + past participle

If the Titanic ***hadn't hit*** *an iceberg, it **wouldn't have sunk**.*
(But it **did** hit an iceberg and it **did** sink.)

*If I**'d known** you were vegetarian, I **wouldn't have cooked** meat.*
(But I didn't know and I cooked you meat.)

2 Match a clause from box A with a clause from box B to make a third conditional sentence.

──── **A** ────
1. If Tess hadn't written a letter,
2. If Angel hadn't gone to Sandbourne,
3. If Alec hadn't provoked her,
4. If Alec had survived,
5. If Angel had written to Tess,

──── **B** ────
A   Tess wouldn't have killed him.
B   she wouldn't have married Alec.
C   Angel wouldn't have returned.
D   he wouldn't have found Tess.
E   Tess wouldn't have been executed.

3 Use the third conditional to write a second sentence which has a similar meaning to the first sentence.

0. I broke my leg skiing. I couldn't go to school.
If I hadn't broken my leg, I would have gone to school.

1. I hurt my hand yesterday. I couldn't play tennis.
If I ....

2. I spent all my money. I couldn't go to the cinema.
If I ....

3. I didn't answer the phone. I didn't know it was you.
I would ....

4. I saved all my money. I bought a DVD player.
If I hadn't ....

5. I didn't study. I didn't pass the exam.
If I ....

6. It rained. We couldn't sit outside.
If it ....

4 Before her execution, Tess wrote one final letter to Angel. Fill the spaces in her letter by putting each verb into the correct tense. Decide if the verb is active/passive or present/past/future.

Dearest Angel,

How are you? I (**0**).*am writing*.. (*write*) this, my last letter, from the prison I (**1**)............... (*take*) to by the police. From my cell I (**2**)............... (*hear*) the bells of the cathedral ringing. Even in this desperate situation I (**3**)............... (*please*) that this ordeal (**4**)............... (*be*) over soon. My only regret, Angel, is that I will never see you again. In what was only a short time together I (**5**)............... (*have*) enough happiness to last a lifetime.

Despite everything the prison is not so bad. The guards (**6**)............... (*be*) very nice to me. One of them (**7**)............... (*bring*) me this paper to write on. I don't have much time but I want you to know that when I (**8**)............... (*take*) from this place tomorrow I (**9**)............... (*think*) of you and your promise to take care of Liza-Lu when I (**10**)............... (*go*). I know you (**11**)............... (*be*) happy together. Until tomorrow at eight.

All my love,

Tess

5 In legal terms it is often said that 'the sentence should fit the crime'. In Tess's case she was executed. Was the sentence correct? What alternative sentences could the judge have given? Which other characters should be punished and what should their sentence be?

6 You have been asked to write a review of *Tess* for a student magazine. Write your review in 120-180 words. Include the following points in your review:

- an introduction which presents your ideas of the story
- a summary of Tess's tragic story – what are the main points of the story?

- an outline of the main characters
- a conclusion which summarises your opinions
- Would you recommend this book? To whom? Why?

STONEHENGE

On the broad expanse of Salisbury Plain in southern England stands a huge stone circle. It was built some time between the Neolithic period and the Bronze Age. This is Stonehenge, the most important prehistoric structure in Europe. Its original purpose remains a mystery, but the site was used for tribal meetings, religious rites, the burial of the dead, and the observation of celestial bodies. [1]

Stonehenge consists of three concentric stone circles. Rectangular sandstone monoliths [2] are arranged in an outer circle 33 metres in diameter and four metres high. The vertical monoliths support others, laid horizontally. Originally, this created a continuous architrave, [3] but only part of it survives today. Within the outer circle is a second circle of smaller blocks. These are a different kind of stone: dolerite, [4] a blue-grey basaltic [5] rock. Inside that is a third circle of ten dolerite pillars, arranged in pairs. Each pair supports an architrave. Within this last circle is the large horizontal block known as the Altar Stone. A path, the 'Avenue', runs across Stonehenge on the north-western side. Beside the Avenue is a horizontal block known as the Slaughter Stone. [6] Opposite that is another called the Heel Stone. This could have been used to determine the summer solstice: [7] on midsummer morning, the sun rises behind the Heel Stone. Stonehenge is surrounded by a circular ditch 104 metres in diameter. The seventeenth-century writer and antiquarian John Aubrey discovered 56 cavities in this ditch, all of which contained the ashes of the cremated dead. These are known as the 'Aubrey Holes'.

1. **celestial bodies** : the sun and the stars.
2. **monoliths** : large blocks.
3. **architrave** : the horizontal blocks formed a continuous 'roof' or beam.
4. **dolerite** : type of rock.
5. **basaltic** : of basalt, a type of dark rock of volcanic origin.
6. **Slaughter Stone** : stone on which things were killed for sacrifice.
7. **solstice** : either of the two times of the year at which the sun is furthest North or South of the equator.

Stonehenge, Salisbury Plain, Wiltshire. Tess was arrested here for the
murder of Alec after she had been briefly reunited with Angel.

Archaeological evidence suggests that Stonehenge was constructed
in several phases. At first there was just the outer circle. Around
2,200 BC, the inner circles were built and the Altar Stone was
placed. The 82 blue dolerite stones that make up the inner circles
were brought from Wales. About 400 burial mounds (2,000-1,500
BC) are situated around Stonehenge. Excavations there have brought
to light [1] precious objects used at funerals. All this testifies to the
social importance of Stonehenge at that time. However, it began to
lose importance as a ceremonial centre after the Bronze Age.
Between 55 BC and 410 AD it was profaned [2] by the Romans, who
knocked down several of the vertical monoliths. In 1797 and 1900,

1. **brought to light** : made something known.
2. **profaned** : treated disrespectfully.

some of the architrave stones fell down, but they were restored to their original places in 1958.

Who built Stonehenge and why? How did they move these massive monoliths? In particular, how did prehistoric people transport the 82 blue stones from Wales, a journey of over 100 kilometres? We may never be able to answer these questions. There are, however, convincing answers to the question of its functions. The Aubrey Holes prove that the place was associated with death and cremation. It may also have been a site of human sacrifice. This supports the idea that one of its functions was religious. But the shape of Stonehenge suggests another more practical use. At various times of the year, the sun and the moon appear between certain stones. Stonehenge can be used to determine when the summer and winter solstices occur and the spring and autumn equinoxes. [1] It can help us predict eclipses of the sun and the moon. Therefore it is very likely that prehistoric astronomy and timekeeping were among its original functions. However, we do not know whether they used the information Stonehenge provided for practical or religious purposes. If they were sun-worshippers, the distinction becomes irrelevant.

Today Stonehenge is a major tourist attraction. A fence was erected around it in the 1970s to prevent people from writing graffiti [2] on the stones. But in the nineteenth century, at the time Tess's story is set, Stonehenge still possessed its original grandeur and mystery. With its associations of sacrifice, death, astronomy, and the distant past, it is the perfect setting for Hardy's great climactic [3] scene.

1. **equinoxes** : the two times of the year (around 21 March and 22 September) when the sun crosses the equator and day and night are of equal length.
2. **graffiti** : drawings or writing on a public wall.
3. **climactic** : intense.

1 Decide if the following statements are true (T) or false (F).

		T	F
1.	Stonehenge is made up of four circles.	☐	☐
2.	It was constructed using a combination of vertical and horizontal blocks of stone.	☐	☐
3.	The monument was built in stages over a period of time.	☐	☐
4.	The Aubrey Holes contained human remains.	☐	☐
5.	The inner circles were built first.	☐	☐
6.	Stonehenge was restored by the Romans.	☐	☐
7.	After the Bronze Age it became a ceremonial centre.	☐	☐
8.	A fence was built around Stonehenge in the 1970s.	☐	☐
9.	Stonehenge can be used to predict eclipses of the sun and moon.	☐	☐
10.	Stonehenge is located in Scotland.	☐	☐

2 Think about the following questions.

- The text tells us that 82 *blue stones* were used in the construction of Stonehenge. These stones came from Wales, a distance of over 100 kilometres. How do you think prehistoric men were able to transport these large and heavy stones over such a long distance?

- Evidence shows that Stonehenge was used as a burial ground. However, historians suggest that the monument was a temple for sun-worshippers. Do you think Stonehenge was used for religious or practical purposes?

- Are there any monuments similar to Stonehenge in your country. Can you describe them? What were they used for?

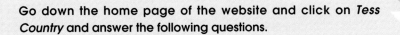

INTERNET PROJECT

Thomas Hardy lived for almost all his life in one of the most beautiful parts of England – Dorset. Let's find out more about Dorset and Thomas Hardy using the Internet.

Go down the home page of the website and click on *Tess Country* and answer the following questions.

1. Describe the Valley of Blackmoor, which is the setting for *Tess of the d'Urbervilles*.
   ....

2. What is the real name for Marlott and the real name of the Pure Drop Pub?
   ....

3. Why is the village famous?
   ....

4. How old is the church in the village and what is its link to *Tess*?
   ....

5. What is the real name of the Valley of Frome in *Tess*?
   ....

6. How old is the real d'Urberville (Turberville) window in the church in Bere Regis (Thomas Hardy's Kingsbere) and what is its link to Tess?
   ....

Don't forget to explore the rest of the website and the other links from the home page.

EXIT TEST

Part 1

READING

1 Look at the text below about Victorian Britain. Choose the most suitable heading from the list A-G for each part 1-6. There is one extra heading which you do not need. An example is provided.

A Worker Migration
B Early Industrialisation
C Difficult Conditions
D Dairy Produce
E Changes in the Law
F Victorian Times
G The Seeds of Change

THE REIGN OF QUEEN VICTORA

0 F

Queen Victoria reigned from 1837 to 1901. During this time Britain went through many changes. In 1837 most people lived in villages and worked on the land. However, by 1901, most lived in towns and worked in offices, shops and factories. It was a time of enormous wealth and industrial progress. A combination of new steam-powered machines and a large number of low paid workers turned out goods and materials cheaper than ever before.

1

Farming methods had changed very little since the 1780s. However they, like everything else in Victorian times, soon began to change. At first the changes were small and the methods very simple. Ploughs were usually pulled by horses and farm labourers had to scatter the seed by hand. Wheat was one of the most common crops and workers cut it with a special tool called a sickle. They beat the wheat to separate the grain from the husks and the straw. Then they ground the grain into flour to make bread.

2

However, soon after the start of Queen Victoria's reign, farmers began to use heavy machinery, particularly steam-powered machines, called traction engines. These were a kind of early tractor with four wheels. They were very powerful and could do the work of seven horses or men. Victorian farmers used them to pull their ploughs across the fields. In the growth and development of Victorian Britain many of the new methods and techniques depended on steam.

3

In some parts of Britain the soil was often too poor for growing crops. Farmers traditionally used this land for sheep and cattle, consequently they did not need the new machines. Farmers usually milked their cows in the fields and then took the milk home in cans that were specially made to fit on their backs. They also used special bowls to separate the cream from the milk. They then turned the cream into butter by shaking it in a simple machine called a churn. Lastly, farmers stamped designs on the butter to show who had made it. These dairy farmers also made cheese. It is a longer process and required that each cheese was squeezed in order to make it firm. This was done using a machine called a press.

4

Farmers who did work the land were often 'tenant farmers.' This meant that they worked the farmland but they didn't own it. During harvest time these farmers used traction engines to provide the power for threshing machines. Workers used large forks to load the machines with the crops that they had cut. The straw and grain were efficiently and mechanically separated. The new machines meant that wealthy farmers employed fewer people. Consequently many villagers had to leave the countryside to find work in the cities.

5

In the cities people often found work in textile mills, which used steam-powered machinery to produce large quantities of material. However, the mills were often dangerous places and mill owners needed large numbers of men, women and children to work in them. At that time there were no laws to protect the workers and no regulations to make sure that workplaces were safe. Housing was usually basic and often overcrowded, sometimes with two or three families sharing one house.

6

In 1848 the government passed the first ever Health Act which meant that local governments or councils took responsibility for work done to improve public health. This covered work such as cleaning the streets, the provision of fresh drinking water and the construction of underground sewerage systems. Some cities also addressed the problem of housing and passed laws that banned the building of houses with outside toilets. Slowly, conditions during Victoria's reign began to improve.

Part 2

WRITING

Answer this question.

1 A penfriend from Canada wants to visit London. He also wants to
see the English countryside. Write a letter of between 120-180 words
including the information about Hardy which you have found out
for your friend.

London
- Hardy's burial place in Poet's Corner, Westminster Abbey, London.
- Places of interest: the National Gallery (portrait of Hardy there) and
  the British Museum.

The Countryside
- Frome Valley, Dorset. The setting for 'Tess of the d'Urbervilles'.
- Stonehenge. Prehistoric monument on Salisbury Plain where Tess was
  captured.
- A day trip to Oxford. The city, which Hardy refers to as Christminster,
  in 'Jude the Obscure'.

Transport & Accommodation
- Accommodation can be expensive. Stay at my flat in London. Get list
  of places to stay in country from tourist office in London.
- Big Bus Company. All connections from London. Prices vary. Credit
  cards accepted.
- Ask for flight details from Canada, so you can meet your pen-friend
  at the airport.

**Write an answer to one of the questions above. Write your answer
in 120 – 180 words.**

2 Write a narrative. The ending of *Tess* is very sad. Imagine you are
the writer. You decide to change the ending. Make it a happy
ending. Begin or end your narrative with the words:

*Angel saw the policemen moving slowly up the hill. He woke Tess
and together, they escaped.*

3 You have been asked to write an article for a magazine with the title: *Tess's life is more difficult than a young person's life today.*

4 Describe an incident in *Tess.* Say what it shows about the characters involved.

Part 3

USE OF ENGLISH

1 For questions 1-15 read the text below and decide which answer (A, B, C or D) best fits each space. There is an example at the beginning (0).

Example: 0. A at   B in   C by   D on

THOMAS HARDY – BIOGRAPHY

Thomas Hardy was born (0).....B..... Dorset in 1840. As he was (1)...........
of nature and the countryside, (2)........... life was the subject of many of
his works. His father, a master-builder, was a fine musician and
transmitted his love for music to his son. (3)........... his mother, was
interested in literature. It was from her that Hardy (4)........... his love for
reading.

Following his father's (5)..........., Hardy chose architecture as a
profession. First (6)........... with a local firm, Hardy later moved to
London in 1862.

While in London he began to (7)........... poems. Unhappy, however,
with both his poetry and his work he returned (8)........... Dorset in 1867.
There he married Emma Gifford, in 1874. In the period (9)........... 1871
to 1897, which is (10)........... to be his first literary period, Hardy
wrote fifteen novels. In his (11)........... novels, irony was the
predominant element. In his later works, he blended this (12)...........
tragedy. During his second period, 1897-1909, Hardy stopped writing
novels. Instead he (13)........... on composing *The Dynasts,* a drama of
verse about the Napoleonic Wars. The third period, from 1909 to his
death, was (14)........... to poetry. In 1912 his first wife died. Two years
later he married his second. He (15)........... the rest of his life in
Dorchester, where he died in 1928.

1.	**A** Like	**B** Keen	**C** Fond	**D** Interested
2.	**A** countryside	**B** nature	**C** season	**D** rural
3.	**A** Although	**B** Instead	**C** But	**D** Contrary
4.	**A** inherited	**B** found	**C** discovered	**D** inspired
5.	**A** model	**B** example	**C** ideas	**D** lesson
6.	**A** works	**B** worked	**C** working	**D** work
7.	**A** writing	**B** wrote	**C** write	**D** written
8.	**A** in	**B** to	**C** at	**D** near
9.	**A** during	**B** of	**C** following	**D** between
10.	**A** considered	**B** consider	**C** think	**D** expected
11.	**A** beginning	**B** initially	**C** firstly	**D** early
12.	**A** in	**B** for	**C** to	**D** with
13.	**A** decided	**B** concentrated	**C** wanted	**D** preferred
14.	**A** devoted	**B** based	**C** concentrated	**D** built
15.	**A** stayed	**B** live	**C** spent	**D** had lived

2 **For questions 1-8 complete the second sentence so that it has a similar meaning to the first. In each case use the word given. You must use between two and five words, including the word given. There is an example at the beginning (0).**

0. 'What a bright colour that machine is,' thought Tess.
   was
   Tess thought *the machine was a very* bright colour.

1. Livestock ate the turnips in the field.
   eaten
   The .... livestock.

2. Tess was the hardest worker in the field.
   than
   No one in .... Tess.

3. The sky was colourless and the field was colourless.
   both
   The sky and the field ....

4. Tess was protected from the wind by a wall of corn.
   protected
   A wall .... the wind.

5. Even though it was cold they worked all day.
fact
Despite .... cold, they worked all day.

6. Tess remembered that the sun hadn't shone since last Sunday, five days ago.
for
The .... five days.

7. In the past turnips were dug up by hand, but not today.
used
Workers .... by hand.

8. When it was dark Tess immediately stopped working.
as
Tess stopped work .... was dark.

3 For questions 1-7 read the text below. Use the word given at the end of each line to form a word that fits in the space in the same line. There is an example at the beginning (0).

As a writer Hardy has often been described as a (0).p̲e̲s̲s̲i̲m̲i̲s̲t̲ .   PESSIMISM
His depressing view of life was due to the intellectual and (1)...................... movements of the time. He was also   SCIENCE
deeply influenced by Darwin's (2)...................... which,   DISCOVER
against all traditional beliefs, showed that the world had existed (3)...................... than man. This led him to refute   LONG
the Bible and its Christian doctrine. Most of his books are set in Wessex, which was one of seven (4)......................   KING
established throughout Britain by early Anglo-Saxons. It provided the ideal location to present what he saw as the consequences of change in agricultural society, as a result of modern (5)...................... . Wessex also provided the   INDUSTRIAL
rural environment and (6)...................... landscapes that   NATURE
Hardy described in such great detail. The presence of nature is an important element of his work. It acts not only as a (7)...................... and a background but as an   SET
essential part of the story.

Tess of the d'Urbervilles

KEY TO THE ACTIVITIES

Page 13 – exercise 1

1. An architect.
2. Darwin's *Origin of the Species* influenced intellectuals of the time with doubts and questions about the origins of the human race.
3. 1867.
4. Hardy published a book every two years and wrote 14 novels, and many volumes of poetry and short stories.
5. *Jude the Obscure*. Both books deal with unusual, for the time, romantic and sexual relationships.
6. Because of the criticism he received for both *Tess* and *Jude*.
7. They did not regard the character of Tess as a pure woman, because she had an illegitimate child. Morality of the time couldn't accept that the mother of an illegitimate child could be 'pure'. Hardy thought, instead, that people should be judged by their intentions.
8. It symbolises the physical love he would offer later.
9. Was Tess's tragedy society's fault or a result of her decadent aristocratic descent?
10. 1928.

Page 14 – exercise 2

1. to the village of 2. Sir John
3. surprised 4. researching the history of the 5. ancient noble
6. a famous knight from 7. amazing
8. extinct 9. marble tombs 10. Pure Drop Pub

Chapter 1

Page 24 – exercise 1

1. He discovered that he came from a noble family.
2. She felt that her father was acting in a ridiculous way.
3. To a village dance.
4. She was thinking about the man who hadn't asked her to dance. (Angel)
5. Jack had drunk too much the night before and was sleeping.
6. She was sleeping.
7. No.
8. Mr Stoke, a successful merchant, changed his name to make it sound more aristocratic.
9. She had an official seal with the family coat of arms on it, and an old silver spoon with the family crest on it.

10. He suggested that Tess should work at the Stoke-d'Urberville family home.

Page 24 – exercise 2

Noun: descendant, nobility, superstition, elegance, surprise, extinction, aristocracy, fool, embarrassment, difficulty
Adjective: descending, noble, superstitious, elegant, surprising, extinct, aristocratic, foolish, embarrassed, difficult

Page 25 – exercise 3

1. descendant (noun)
2. noble (adjective)
3. aristocracy (noun)
4. elegant (adjective)
5. embarrassed (adjective)
6. foolish (adjective)
7. extinct (adjective)
8. superstition (noun)
9. surprise (noun)
10. difficulties (noun)

Page 26 – exercise 4

1. Jack Durbeyfield was told by Parson Tringham that he was…
2. Tess was encouraged to see…
3. Tess was met by a young man…

Page 26 – exercise 5

1. was looked at   2. taken home from the   3. was said to be   4. fun of by the girls   5. was embarrassed by Jack's   6. was standing   7. was chosen to   8. were sung by Tess's   9. was penetrated by   10. was changed to sound

Chapter 2

Page 40 – exercise 1

1. To earn money to buy her family a new horse.
2. Because her best clothes over emphasised her figure.
3. The fact that Tess had laughed at her.
4. She blushed.
5. Because Tess had escaped one difficult situation only to find herself in a more difficult situation.
6. As it was a nice night he wanted to ride longer.
7. He gave her father a new horse.
8. She was sad and began to cry.
9. To get a better view of the countryside.
10. Tess's innocence was in need of protection.

Page 40 – exercise 2

	carriage	horse	car	bicycle	bus	plane
get in	✓	✗	✓	✗	✗	✗
ride	✗	✓	✗	✓	✗	✗
get on	✗	✓	✗	✓	✓	✓
drive	–	✗	✓	✗	✓	✗
miss	✗	✗	✗	✗	✓	✓
catch	✗	✗	✗	✗	✓	✓

Page 40 – exercise 3

1. get on **2.** missed **3.** ride **4.** get in
5. catch **6.** drive

Page 41 – exercise 4

1. in **2.** around **3.** off **4.** up **5.** in
6. by **7.** on **8.** of **9.** on **10.** about

Page 42 – exercise 5

1. **D** drove/paid
2. **E** descended/went
3. **F** walked/saw
4. **A** rode/held
5. **C** climbed/waited
6. **B** rode/began

Page 42 – exercise 6

1. As/While he was working, she was lying on the beach.
2. As/While I was waiting for the bus, it started to rain.
3. As/While they were walking down the street, they saw an accident.
4. As/While we were driving home last night, we listened to the radio.
5. As I entered the house, the alarm went off.
6. While we were at the check in, our plane took off.

Page 44 – exercise 3

1. T **2.** F **3.** F **4.** T **5.** F **6.** T

Chapter 3

Page 51 – exercise 1

1. F – It seemed more beautiful than usual.
2. F – She had no fear of him.
3. F – He asked her why she was crying.
4. T
5. F – She stood passively.
6. F – The message seemed. frightening and horrible.
7. T
8. T
9. F – She hated the way they looked at her.
10. F – She felt that she was guilty.

Page 51 – exercise 2

1. heaviest **2.** material **3.** sorrow
4. married **5.** admire **6.** frequently
7. guilt

Page 51 – exercise 3

1. the largest **2.** real **3.** sadness
4. in a couple **5.** respect **6.** often
7. responsibility

Page 52 – exercise 4

1. I won't come back
2. … I did not go there because I loved you
3. I don't want your money
4. … didn't you think of your family
5. You should have been more careful
6. why she had run away
7. she wished she had never been born
8. that she would never love him
9. she had come home to be married
10. why she hadn't warned her

Page 54 – exercise 1

1. warm **2.** easy **3.** been **4.** on
5. that **6.** field **7.** of **8.** out
9. move **10.** other **11.** cut
12. smaller **13.** behind **14.** into
15. interesting **16.** becomes

Chapter 4

Page 60 – exercise 1

1. Approximately ten months. (October-August)
2. The morning mists evaporated. It awoke those still sleeping.
3. Hats to protect against the sun and gloves to prevent their hands being scratched.
4. Her sisters and brothers.
5. She thought the story about the woman in The Chase was a sad one.
6. Tess felt happy about the friendliness shown by the other women.
7. Weak, small and ill.
8. The baby hadn't been baptised.
9. So she could wake her brothers and sisters.
10. Because she was filled with the faith of her religion.

Page 60 – exercise 2

1. D 2. E 3. H 4. I 5. A 6. J
7. B 8 F 9. C 10. G

Page 61 – exercise 3

1. entered the field
2. tying the corn
3. wore hats
4. raised her eyes
5. unfastened the front of her dress
6. to feel a little
7. lit a candle
8. looked tall

Page 63 – exercise 3

1. winter
2. simple girl
3. complex woman
4. soul
5. her sorrows
6. feeling of germination
7. be comfortable in Marlott again
8. heard
9. many miles to the south
10. hope

Chapter 5

Page 70 – exercise 1

1. She was filled with a desire for life.
2. Because she blamed them for all her troubles.
3. He asked her if she wanted something to eat before starting to work.
4. At a dance in Marlott.
5. Because he had refused to become a parson.
6. Because he was disgusted with the city.
7. He was 26.
8. He liked them. 'He liked the farm workers and took an interest in their characters and beliefs'.
9. Because everyone, including Angel, was listening to her.
10. He thought of her more than the others.

Page 70 – exercise 2

1. complex 2
2. took 8
3. hired 3
4. brightest 7
5. noticed 9
6. watched 5
7. wondered 6
8. excitement 4
9. observe 10
10. through 1

Page 72 – exercise 3

1. defining
2. non-defining – The cart passed by Kingsbere Church, where the d'Urbervilles were buried.
3. non-defining – It is like a story from medieval times, when faith was a living thing.
4. defining
5. non-defining – Tess went to bed in a large room over the milk-house, which she shared with three other milkmaids.
6. defining
7. defining

Page 72 – exercise 4

a. She heard of a dairy farm *which* needed a milk maid.
b. He returned to the countryside *where* he decided to learn all aspects of farming.
c. That young man, *who* plays the harp, is milking a cow.
d. Tess decided to go somewhere else *where* no one knew her history.
e. Tess returned to her family, *where* she stayed all through the winter.
f. Tess was milking the cow, *when* she heard a voice ask 'why?'

Page 73 – exercise 2

1. F 2. F 3. T 4. F 5. T 6. F

Chapter 6

Page 84 – exercise 1

1. c 2. d 3. b 4. c 5. d 6. b 7. a
8. d 9. c 10. b

Page 86 – exercise 2

Possible answers:

Alec	Tess	Angel
quick-tempered	confused	clever
reckless	naive	gentle
deceitful	hardworking	rebellious

Page 86 – exercise 4

1. clever 2. naive 3. handsome
4. guilty 5. deceitful 6. rebellious

Page 87 – exercise 5

1. G (first conditional)
2. D (first conditional)
3. E (second conditional)
4. A (zero conditional)
5. C (second conditional)
6. H (first conditional)
7. F (zero conditional)
8. B (second conditional)

No Sex, Please, We're Victorians!

Page 91 – exercise 1

1. masters 2. censored 3. deleted
4. ostracised 5. banned 6. explicit
7. instalments 8. illegitimate
9. offensive 10. expurgated
11. condemned 12. hypocrisy

Page 92 – exercise 2

1. B 2. A 3. B 4. B 5. A 6. B

Chapter 7

Page 104 – exercise 1

1. F 2. T 3. F 4. F 5. T 6. F 7. T
8. F 9. F 10. T

Page 105 – exercise 2

1. don't think he should
2. think she should tell Angel
3. shouldn't have embraced
4. think they should have agreed

Page 106 – exercise 3

1. must tell
2. mustn't ask me
3. had to write
4. will have to tell/confess

Page 106 – exercise 4

1. have to **2.** must **3.** must
4. have to **5.** have to **6.** must

Page 106 – exercise 5

1. C must **2.** D should **3.** B should
4. A must

Page 108 – exercise 1

1. who **2.** ✓ **3.** not **4.** it **5.** ✓ **6.** of
7. ✓ **8.** ✓ **9.** ✓ **10.** then **11.** out
12. ✓ **13.** ✓ **14.** much **15.** too
16. ✓ **17.** ✓

Chapter 8

Page 122 – exercise 1

1. He had imagined Tess to be one thing. The reality was another thing.
2. Divorce.
3. Tess's was passionate. Angel's was idealistic.
4. So she wouldn't disgrace him or her future child.
5. Tess as a wife was dead.
6. Because Angel had shown tenderness.
7. To start a farm.
8. She had no job. She sent her last money to her family.

9. Marian, one of the milkmaids at Talbothay's, told her.
10. Because it was the man Angel had hit.

Page 122 – exercise 2

A 1. Tess **2.** Reverend Clare
   3. Joan **4.** Angel **5.** Jack
   6. Mrs d'Urberville **7.** Jack
B 1. Tess **2.** Angel **3.** Angel
   4. Marian **5.** Joan **6.** The Reverend Clare **7.** Alec **8.** Jack **9.** Alec

Page 123 – exercise 3

A 1. d **2.** a **3.** f **4.** g **5.** h **6.** b
   7. e **8.** c
B 1. Angel left the room because Tess had burst into tears.
   2. Angel turned away because Tess had offered him her lips.
   3. Tess's heart was hungry for love because Angel had been cold to her for some days.
   4. Tess couldn't deceive him because he had been so good to her.
   5. Tess found work in another village because she had left Marlott again.
   6. Tess sent money to her family because her mother had written a letter saying they couldn't pay their debts.
   7. No one answered the door because they had gone to church.

Page 125 – exercise 1

1. back **2.** crowd **3.** asked
4. replied **5.** but **6.** hear **7.** was
8. own **9.** greatest **10.** met **11.** had
12. up **13.** more **14.** through
15. beating

Chapter 9

Page 137 – exercise 1

1. Who convinced Alec to repent? *Reverend Clare.*
2. How did Alec react when he saw Tess? *His lips trembled and his eyes avoided hers.*
3. Why did Tess not believe that Alec had repented? *Because Angel did not believe in religion.*
4. What was the meaning of the stone pillar? *It is a bad omen. A monument to someone who was hanged there.*
5. What did Alec want to do in Africa? *He wanted to be a missionary.*
6. What made Tess write to Angel? *Because she felt threatened and tempted by the presence of Alec.*
7. Why was Angel not happy with his new life? *Physically he had been ill. Emotionally he missed Tess.*
8. Why did Tess's family leave the cottage? *Because when Jack died the family were not allowed to stay.*
9. What is the legend of the d'Urberville coach? *A 16th century d'Urberville tried to escape with a beautiful woman. In the struggle someone was killed. The coach is a bad omen.*
10. Who did Tess and her family find lying on the tomb? *Alec d'Urberville.*

Page 137 – exercise 2

1. AL 2. T 3. AL 4. AN 5. T 6. JK 7. J 8. AL 9. LL 10. J

Page 138 – exercise 3

1. E 2. F 3. G 4. D 5. B 6. A

Page 140 – exercise 2

1. anxious 2. older 3. Christian 4. discouraging 5. dignified 6. separation 7. absence 8. lovely 9. born 10. dead

Chapter 10

Page 150 – exercise 1

1. F 2. T 3. T 4. F 5. F 6. T 7. F 8. T 9. T 10. F

Page 151 – exercise 2

1. C 2. D 3. A 4. E 5. B

Page 151 – exercise 3

1. If I hadn't hurt my hand yesterday, I could have played tennis.
2. If I hadn't spent all my money, I could have gone to the cinema.
3. I would have answered the phone, if I had known it was you.
4. If I hadn't saved all my money, I wouldn't have bought a DVD player.
5. If I had studied, I would have passed my exam.
6. If it hadn't rained, we could have sat outside.

Page 152 – exercise 4

1. was taken 2. can hear 3. am pleased 4. will be 5. had 6. have been 7. brought 8. am taken 9. will be 10. am gone 11. will be

Stonehenge

Page 156 – exercise 1

1. F 2. T 3. T 4. T 5. F 6. F 7. F 8. T 9. T 10. F

PART 1 – READING

1

1. G   2. B   3. D   4. A   5. C   6. E

PART 3 – USE OF ENGLISH

1

1. C   2. D   3. B   4. A   5. B   6. C
7. C   8. B   9. D   10. A   11. D
12. D   13. B   14. A   15. C

2

1. turnips were eaten by the
2. the field worked harder than

3. were both colourless
4. of corn protected Tess from
5. the fact that it was/it being
6. sun hadn't shone for
7. used to dig up turnips
8. as soon as it

3

1. scientific
2. discoveries
3. longer
4. kingdoms
5. industrialisation
6. natural
7. setting

NOTES

NOTES

Black Cat English Readers

BLACK CAT ENGLISH CLUB
Membership Application Form

BLACK CAT ENGLISH CLUB is for those who love English reading and seek for better English to share and learn with fun together.

Benefits offered: *- Membership Card*   *- English learning activities*

- Book discount coupon   *- Black Cat English Reward Scheme*

- English learning e-forum   *- Surprise gift and more...*

Simply fill out the application form below and fax it back to 2565 1113 or send it back to the address at the back.

Join Now! It's FREE exclusively for readers who have purchased *Black Cat English Readers* !

(Please fill out the form with **BLOCK LETTERS**.)

The title of Black Cat English Reader/book set that you have purchased: _____

English Name: _____ (Surname) _____ (Given Name)

Chinese Name: _____

Address: |_|_|_|_|_|_|_|_|_|_|_|_|_|_|_|_|_|_|_|_|_|_|_|_|_|_|_|_|_|_|_|_|_|_|_|_|

|_|_|_|_|_|_|_|_|_|_|_|_|_|_|_|_|_|_|_|_|_|_|_|_|_|_|_|_|_|_|_|_|_|_|_|_|

|_|_|_|_|_|_|_|_|_|_|_|_|_|_|_|_|_|_|_|_|_|_|_|_|_|_|_|_|_|_|_|_|_|_|_|_|

Tel: _____   Fax: _____

Email: _____

(Login password for e-forum will be sent to this email address.)

Sex: ❑ Male   ❑ Female

Education Background: ❑ Primary 1-3   ❑ Primary 4-6   ❑ Junior Secondary Education (F1-3)

❑ Senior Secondary Education (F4-5)   ❑ Matriculation

❑ College   ❑ University or above

Age: ❑ 6 - 9   ❑ 10 - 12   ❑ 13 - 15   ❑ 16 - 18   ❑ 19 - 24   ❑ 25 - 34

❑ 35 - 44   ❑ 45 - 54   ❑ 55 or above

Occupation: ❑ Student   ❑ Teacher   ❑ White Collar   ❑ Blue Collar

❑ Professional   ❑ Manager   ❑ Business Owner   ❑ Housewife

❑ Others (please specify: _____)

As a member, what would you like **BLACK CAT ENGLISH CLUB** to offer:

❑ Member gathering/ party   ❑ English class with native teacher   ❑ English competition

❑ Newsletter   ❑ Online sharing   ❑ Book fair

❑ Book discount   ❑ Others (please specify: _____)

Other suggestions to **BLACK CAT ENGLISH CLUB**: _____

_____

Please sign here: _____   (Date: _____)

Visit us at Quality English Learning Online http://publish.commercialpress.com.hk/qel

Stamp
Here

BLACK CAT ENGLISH CLUB
The Commercial Press (Hong Kong) Ltd.
9/F, Eastern Central Plaza,
3 Yiu Hing Road, Shau Kei Wan,
Hong Kong